MARKED ONES
THEODOR AND AIDAN
BY
JULIA MATTHEWS

Publisher Note

This is a work of fiction. Names, characters, places, and events are from the author's imagination or used fictitiously. Any resemblance to actual events or person, living or dead, is purely coincidental.

Cover Design by Oliviaprodesign

Prologue

Aidan

"You can't do it this way."

My words were futile, but I had to voice my concerns. More like fear of what would take place if Lord Tang continue down his path. I know Rex screwed up. Broke all kinds of Lord Tang's rules. He deserved what he got, but what Lord Tang planned would break his word and rules. Put all his subject in jeopardy of punishment. None of us deserved that. Yet . . .

"Do not tell me what I can do." Lord Tang pressed in on me, drawing a hiss from me.

"You best watch yourself, Aidan."

Lord Tang had a point. I was his second. I did as told. All of Lord Tang's subjects did. Did not matter if one of us doubted his logic or action. What bothered me most was that all of this could have been avoided.

"It is the only way for us to keep track of what is going on with these Bombardians."

I agreed we needed to know more about the race that Rex uncovered, but . . . "Is there not another way you could address the issue? Maybe go back to speak with the gentlemen you spoke to the other day."

Lord Tang lifted his hand, pulling it back but the blow never came. Thank goodness. Lord Tang's claws had glistened as the sun reflected off them.

"You do as I say. That is your job, or do I need to find another second."

"No, Sir." I'd been at Lord Tang's side for over forty years. What it took to get the position sickened me, but I did it, just like I would do as Lord Tang bid. "Have you planted the seed?"

"Course I have."

Wasted breath. That's all I'd done. That and riled up my leader. All that was left to do was wait for the backfire.

Chapter 1

Theodor

"Lord Tang would not dare lie to any Bombardian."

Shit. "Did you say Lord?"

Why . . . What was that . . . Fuck. Blood Drinker. Uncle Robert and I made a promise to him. We upheld it. Far as I'd known Uncle Robert informed his fellow Royal Leaders. He'd told Lord Tang he would fill in his four cousins, the other leaders of the Bombardians. Uncle Robert had left me in charge of Uncle Alvin in order to inform them of the attack on his brother. An attack on any Bombardian was horrible, but one on a royal blood carrier was horrific. It would have taken an extremely strong person to take down a Bombardian. We all had enhanced strengths, but a royal blood carrier held more than others. Uncle Alvin held a small amount of royal blood, but it still boosted his strength. Not as much as it did his brothers and me.

Anthony glanced my way as I came to stand beside him. "You heard of Lords before?"

Hadn't he? Fact of Blood Drinkers would have been taught to him while he . . . Right. Anthony paid little to no attention to his lessons. It wasn't my right to tell him. I couldn't. I'd made a promise to Uncle Robert, who was a Royal Leader at the time, and no Bombardian broke their word to a leader. Not even a current leader like me. What was I to do? Lying to my cousins did not rank high on my list. Never made it on it. Why would it, they would know the moment it left my mouth. What did I do?

Vagueness.

Sourness consumed my mouth and burned as I swallowed before I answered Anthony.

"Folklore story my Uncle told me about."

"Same Uncle that was sent into hiding?"

"Yep."

"Looks like you'll be going on a hunt as well."

I would, but not for my Uncle. Might have to contact him, but I would not do so until I had to.

"Uh . . . What did I miss?" Franklin walked up to my side.

"You ever heard of Lords?" Anthony's crackling voice showed how much he longed to be in the fold. Made me sorry for him.

"Only in human history books." Franklin leaned forward and nailed me with a look that demanded explanation. "What's he going on about?"

Shit. Fuck. Franklin didn't know either. Uncle Robert left Uncle Alvin in my care so he could tell the others. Had he . . . Damn it.

Shit. Damn. Hell. What a cluster fuck.

The entire Bombardian world had been told Uncle Robert and two other Royal Leaders had been killed. Not the case. Uncle Robert and the other two had found their Keeper. The two remaining Royal Leaders decided it was foul, or something, so they exiled them. Not that they had the right to do so. Royal Leaders go on majority rule and two votes for exile would not have carried the votes. Uncle Robert and the others said they agreed with their bigoted cousins to keep the peace. Ensure stability among the Bombardians. Stupid on their part. About as bad as thinking Uncle Robert and the other two had decided to search out Lord Tang and engaged in fight, losing. I'd assumed wrong. I believed the other remaining leaders told the new leaders, and their future successors, about the Blood Drinkers. Such thoughts were why I had not verified that Uncle Robert told the others when they came to us a few months back.

"See . . . None of you know what you are facing." Gobbler's chuckle sickened me, but part of his words sounded like truth. If my cousins did not know about Lord Tang and the Blood Drinker race, then . . . darkness clung over them. Not quite as much as me, but Uncle Robert and I got very little information from Lord Tang. "I can't wait for him to come for us."

"Come for you?" Theodor snorted. "He will not get into this house."

Chapter 2

Theodor

I was the eldest Royal Leader, which meant I led. Normally. Anthony had his mind set on going to his ex-lover, so I let him. Not without a bit of a grumbling about my dislike. Still my full focus wasn't on the matter at hand, so it might have been best to let one of the others lead. Anthony wouldn't have been my choice, but he was why the situation arose. Right then, all I could think about was figuring out how to get around my promise to Uncle Robert and Lord Tang. Lying to my cousins would not work and . . . I would not do so. Uncle Robert had not promised to tell the other Royal Leaders. That meant . . . I could enlighten them as much as . . . Okay, I would keep as much as I could to myself until I had to . . .

"What is a Lord?"

"Pretty much what you read about in paranormal romance fictions."

"Vampires?" Franklin's choice of words fit, but wrong. They were Blood Drinkers, but Vampire fit them. "Theodor, you've lost your mind."

"Has he?" Anthony's questions had me quirking an eyebrow. "Some would consider us werewolves. We have a wolf inside. Does that make us fictional?"

"No, but . . . Okay, Let's say Vampires are real. Why would one attack us?"

Good question. One I had no answer to, but I would find one. I got two feet before an arm blocked my path.

"Do you know what they are capable of?"

Knew some. Not much, but . . . They had not been told and had the right to know. Uncle would not want me to keep facts from them. I was sure he would have told the other leaders if they had not faked his death.

I shook my head.

"What all did your Uncle tell you about them?"

I knew little, but I'd fudge on the truth earlier and would not backtrack. "They survive on blood. Few left. The ones left are old and dangerous."

"Dangerous?" Franklin hugged and rolled his eyes, making me push down a chuckle. "Course they are. They drink blood."

"He meant to us as well."

Anthony was smarter than he gave himself credit for.

"Yep." I sighed. "We were . . . Interrupted before he could tell me more. The Awakening." Not a lie. Uncle Robert would have told me more about what him and Lord Tang discussed during their time in the woods once his cousins knew everything. That I was sure of. Right then all I wanted was to know what Anthony knew about the situation at hand. I knocked his arm from me and demanded to know what he knew.

Next few minutes were a bit tense. I was sure Anthony and me might have come to blows if David had not showed up pissed about having to enter his house through the front door. Not that he didn't have the right to be ticked off. He'd left his sick Keeper in our protection and his house had been invaded. It hadn't bothered Bryan in any manner, but that would not matter to David. And it should not.

What bothered me most was that there was anguish in David's eyes and all over his face. It scared me. He'd left to find out what was wrong with his Keeper, the calmer of his beast, and came back with . . . Had he found out there was something that could eliminate the life of a Keeper?

I remained quiet and listened as Anthony all but begged for David to explain what was wrong with Bryan. I wasn't sure if Anthony would have gotten his request if his Keeper had not come upstairs and demanded an answer. What we got was a bit more than shocking. Amazing. Shocking.

Who would have thought a man could . . . Shit. Major situation came from such a joyous condition. No one would have considered such an intense connection could form between an unborn child and a father. Appeared that a Keeper and Royal Leader's relationship was much stronger than thought. More in-depth than Uncle Robert, Uncle Tray, and . . . What was Caleb's Uncle's name? Crap, my mind was bouncing around and around so fast making my head spin, causing my breathing to falter.

Heat sored around me as I forced air through my lungs. Okay, the three exiled Uncles had not told us everything about pregnant Keepers. Current and ex Royal Leaders would have to discuss that. Then again . . . It was David's fault. All four of ours. David had not wanted to discuss it before his Pledging Ceremony. We had promised to get the information from them but failed to do so.

Stupid on all our parts. From the sound of it, Bryan was in for a long hard road. Not only was he expecting, but twins. Twins that him and David were connected to in such a deep manner that it seemed unreal. Okay, it was unreal and never heard of. Just like . . .

My cousin's lack of knowledge of Lord Tang and Blood Drinkers. More upheaval awaited my cousins if I did not figure out what Lord Tang was up to. How did I do that if I did not know how to contact him?

A problem that could wait until Anthony gathered information from his ex-lover. Until then . . . I split my mind in two directions. The display Anthony and his Keeper put on in front of Anthony's ex-lover and my cousins' lack of knowledge.

Splitting my mind did not work out too well for me, because before I knew it the hallways was full of . . . Oh crap. What was . . . What was up with my body? Why was my cock throbbing when the hallway was full of . . . Blood Drinkers? Worse, Lord Tang.

Chapter 3

Aidan

My heart plummeted as my dick hardened.

Didn't need to second-guess myself. Knew who the tall, bulky, shiny dark haired man was. Never seen him a day in my life, but I knew him. Wanted to know more about him. Everything.

Aidan, pay attention. There are a lot of Bombardians swarming in.

From a quick count there were at least twenty storming the hallway. More crowding the stairs. All bulky, but none held a candle to the dark haired man. He oozed with power and strength. The ones swarming around the small group of men screamed, "Guards."

The guy I seek is here.

Which one? Was he the tall hunk that I'd learn all about?

He stands in the middle with a bit of fear seeping from him. I did not think I scared him when he was younger.

Bet he had. No matter how much power and strength you grown into, things from your childhood stuck with you and Lord Tang was overwhelming to most people. He expected obedience from all. Such an attitude would not have gone over well with a Bombardian leader, or as Lord Tang called them, Commanders.

Keep your eye on the tall one in the middle, but make sure the others have their eyes on those guards.

Tall . . . Middle. Shit. He'd been the youngster Lord Tang interacted with. Crap. This was no . . . Oh boy. Precautions had to be taken.

Half a blink of an eye and a mental brick barricade had been thrown up between me and Lord Tang. Did not need him knowing what was going on. Not yet. Had to . . . What? There was something . . . I'd never heard of a Blood Drinker being paired with . . . Not that it mattered. I knew who stood across from me. No way I'd let my Inamorato slip through my hands. They were rare. Real rare. Things had to be played right, or . . . Research was required. Inquiries need to be made before . . .

Part of me feared what my body and heart told me. There was no hard proof that a Bombardian could be an Inamorato, the other half to a Blood Drinker.

An elbow landed against my ribs as Lord Tang spoke to the group he'd came seeking. He'd gone the wrong way about getting in touch with the Bombardian he interacted with all those years ago. Everything he done since he met those two Bombardians had been . . . Wrong. There'd been no reason to insert his will on the men he had. They'd been . . . Sick. Twisted. Had a personal agenda of their own. That's what had made them easy prey for Lord Tang. Yet . . . Things still became a mess thanks to Lord Tang not keeping a strong hold on the men. One had decided he controlled the others and used it to gain his own goal. Lord Tang had all the control and would make sure that the ones who disobeyed him were punished. The entire situation unfolding, could have been avoided if Lord Tang had done as I suggested. Retraced his steps through the woods and sought out the two Bombardians he met. He swore doing so showed weakness. Just another issue I disagreed with Lord Tang on. Seeking aid did not make one look weak, it showed strength and smarts.

Will you pay attention, Aidan?

Crap. I'd let my mind barrier slip. Couldn't do that if I did not want Lord Tang to pick up on the fact that a Bombardian was my other half. Question was . . . How would the Bombardian take to it? Did he feel the same connection that most Inamorato felt towards us? Would he seek me out if he did?

"My task has been accomplished."

Lord Tang snapped his fingers and faded away, leaving me to ensure the rest followed suit. One by one the others used their magic to take them back to the safety of the domain. I was the last to leave and did so with reluctance. Leaving my other half had me pressing my hand against my chest to ensure there was no hole. No hole, but I knew the feeling would only get bigger as I faded back to my homeland. I had no choice. I had to let things play out. Find out if he would come to me, or answer Lord Tang's message. If he could figure out what my Lord wanted. Message wasn't clear, but Lord Tang swore the man would understand. I hoped so. More for me than for my Lord. Although . . . Once he discovered that a Marked One lived among Lord Tang's domain he would not be rushing to leave. Nope. He'd aid his subject, like any good leader would.

With regret I chanted the spell that would take me home.

Chapter 4

Theodor

Lord Tang and his Blood Drinkers did not belong in the same house as my cousins and their Keepers. Nope. Him and his guys needed to scoot.

I went to lunge, but my feet were weighted into place. Just like it'd been years ago when I first saw Uncle Alvin. I'd been a boy then. Knew enough to know I never wanted to interact with the monster again, yet . . . He was feet from me. Wasn't a kid anymore. Time I stepped up and done what needed doing. Protecting. Guarding. Leading. Meant lots of explaining later.

Time my mind put my mouth to work. Best option I had was to help Anthony and Franklin spin the tale they were in the midst of.

"They didn't do their job." Thank the heavens. I sounded stronger than I was.

"That's why they were so freaked about Lord Tang coming."

The ten Bombardians who invaded Anthony's Keeper's bedroom pissed off the wrong being. Lord Tang wasn't someone you wanted an enemy out of. I knew that from the first time I seen him. He had an air of authority and superiority. Neither was conducive to screwing around with.

"Sure was, Franklin. They knew we could protect them best from the monster they got into bed with."

A faint growl slipped from me, thankfully, it came out stronger than I felt. Wasn't sure why the weakness was plaguing me. I did. I knew little about the Blood Drinkers and that scared me. But I had to do what had to be done, so I moved to Anthony's side. Too bad I took a huge step back a second later. Damn it. I was the eldest Royal Leader. I had to step up and do what was best for my people. To aid my cousins. If I'd believed that, I would have told my cousins the truth about Lord Tang from the get-go.

"They fear," Kevin's words where muffled from the wall of water Anthony created around him. For someone who barely knew his affinity, he'd conjured up a great barrier. Too bad, it didn't keep Kevin's ass quiet. "My reaction when Lord Tang releases me."

"You sure he will?"

Anthony's Keeper sure had courage to stand up and speak his mind, but I feared him doing so. He might have been a bit afraid as well. His head was pressed into Anthony's neck. Wrong. He whispered to Anthony. "He knows more than he told you."

Boy did I. Didn't have me speaking up, though. I just kept listening.

"Sure does, honey."

"Do you know what's up with him?"

"No. He's not acting like himself. That's for sure."

Course my cousins caught onto my unusual reaction. They knew me as good as I knew them. Even the two newest ones knew enough about me to know I was acting out of the norm.

"My task," the newcomer's words ruffled through the air as he evaporated into a blue haze that trickled into nothingness. "Has been accomplished."

What did that mean? What had Lord Tang done, besides scare me. Not so much fear. Okay, fear. How could it not be? His voice ripped a long ago memory from my core. Brought a little scared boy to life. One that I'd buried long ago and promised to keep hidden. Just like I'd been able to do. Like I promised to do. Little I could do to . . .

Ah shit. That was it. Lord Tang hadn't been trying to harm us. Nope. He'd been trying to get a message to the ones who knew his kind existed. Why though? What did he need our help with? He was more powerful than us. Or was he? Sure seemed like it years ago, but . . . I'd been a boy who'd saw his Uncle after a brutal attack. Damn it. The man had different abilities than my kind, but he was not stronger than us. Not me. Nope. I would not tolerate him being so. Nope. I would not tolerate him coming into my cousin's home to deliver a message when all he had to do was pick up a damn phone. I guess his people had phones. Oh well, there were better ways to get a message than to make it look like an enemy had come knocking. Then again . . . Maybe one had. If so . . . I was going to eliminate it before it harmed anymore of my people.

All that remained in the hallway was two of my cousins and a bunch of Combatants. If Lord Tang had a message he wanted delivered, then I'd let him. Afterward, I'd have to come ask for forgiveness from my cousins.

I hated apologizes. Oh well, best to ask for forgiveness than to break a non-written truce.

I pointed at the wall of the water and said, "You know he's not coming to release any of you." Lord Tang would kill them first. Not that I cared. Those men had turned on their own kind. They deserved death. "Leave him locked in by water."

I almost laughed at the huge eyes Franklin gave me. Guess I'd be making them even bigger when I gave my next order, because I knew not one of them would follow it. "Tell your Combatants to leave."

My heart skipped two beats for every one it took. Pounding consuming my head as memories rushed to life, making my stomach churn. I could all but hear Uncle Alvin's screams as he ran from the edge of the woods shouting for my Uncle Robert. His flawless, baby skin held four claw marks. Uncle Robert took off running with me behind him, even though he told me to remain in the shed. My little mind had come to life with what I was supposed to do as the next in-line to take the Royal Leaders spot. First thought that came to mind was that a Mélange had escaped a confinement house and attacked him. The closer I got the scene changed. Blood oozed from Uncle Alvin's throat, soaking his white and blonde hair. I froze for a couple of heartbeats, letting the fear wash over me. It took hard work to shove it aside, sort of like I'd done earlier, but I managed to do it.

My mind kicked into gear and the finer aspect of being a Royal Leader came rushing back to life. Not like it'd been far from mind. It had been what me and Uncle Robert had been discussing. I yanked the shirt over my head just as Uncle Alvin collapsed.

Uncle Robert laid him on the ground and pressed my shirt to his neck as his dead like stare landed on me. Scared me worse than the sight in front of me, but what he said had me falling into some kind of statue.

"Theodor, it's time to put your Royal Leaders talents to work."

I questioned what he meant for about half a second then realized he meant my affinity. Fire. Once on my knees I shoved the shirt aside and rested my hand over Uncle Alvin's mangled neck.

Heat zoomed through my chest, down my arms, and into my hand. A straight line of fire flowed from the center of my palm, cauterizing the two huge tears in my Uncle's neck.

Cotton might as well clung to the roof of my mouth. Horrifying silent roars and demands for an explanation filled my mind. Took me two attempts before I managed to ask Uncle Robert who stabbed Uncle Alvin with a fork. Uncle Robert shook his head and motioned for me to slip under Uncle Alvin. With sharp short words he told me to stay with Uncle Alvin.

He was off and into the woods before I could take another breath. Felt like hours passed instead of twenty minutes. Uncle Robert and some bald headed man walked out of the edge of the woods. Uncle Robert's downcast lip and fisted hands had me stiffening and seeping into the deepest part of my soul to gain access to Fire. If I had managed it a five hundred degree of fire would have flowed through the newcomer. One shake of Uncle Robert's head had me standing down.

The rest of the night came to life in a vivid flash.

"Thought you said we would be alone." A deep rich voice flowed from the stranger like music from a record player.

"This is one of our future leaders. He will keep your secret, will you not Young Theodor?"

Uncle Robert's stern expression told me I would go along with the show unfolding.

"I will do what is best for my kind at all times, Commander Robert."

Robert nodded, but the guy beside him grunted and tilted his head. "This is a young leader of yours, Commander Robert?"

"It is."

"He is going to be strong. One I believe will do as he says, but his answer leaves him many ways to relive himself of such a burden."

I knew how to word things so I had a back door to slip through. I'd been an idiot if I hadn't. And no Royal Leader, future or present, were such.

"I will accept him at his word and leave it at that. I am sure he will not reveal my secret to anyone unless it is necessary. In return, I will ensure no more of my kind makes it onto your area, or attacks any of your kind. I see no reason for us to interact at all. Is that not right, Commander Robert?"

"It is."

Tightness clung to Uncle Robert's voice, showing his distaste. Not shocking. Uncle Robert disliked secrets, but Bombardians had more than their fair share.

"Then let me assist your brother, Commander Robert."

Uncle Robert motioned for me to put Uncle Alvin down and back up. One step back was all I took. Would not leave my Uncle Alvin unguarded from someone I knew nothing about. I did not trust the stranger further than I could stretch my arms.

"He escaped my child before he drank too much." The rich deep voice guy said. "All he will need is some juice." The guy looked up at me and stood. "What did you use to seal the teeth holes."

Teeth? What in the world?

Uncle Robert rolled his eyes at me, telling me my mouth hung open like I expected. His displeasure at my lack of control was beyond clear. Took all I could do to shrug at him, but the facts remained the same. The man said those holes were teeth marks. I knew no way anyone could manage to bite someone in the neck and leave such marks. Not a human at least. Not a true . . . Hold up a minute.

"He's not human." I moved in front of Uncle Alvin. "What did you do to my Uncle?"

"Young Theodor," Uncle Robert moved in front of me, cupping my chin. "You know I would not have brought danger to my land and family. Do you not?"

I nodded.

"Then you know this man did not do this to your Uncle."

I nodded again.

"I will fill you in on the details after our company has taken his leave."

"Yes, Commander Robert."

"Good. Stand down. Let him finish explaining what will help Alvin."

I stepped back but remained on high alert. Something about the man . . . Disturbed me. Put fear in me. But . . . Intrigued me.

"The young man will be fine. Some juice and extra rest." The man stepped back and held his hand out to Uncle Robert, who shook it. The guy shifted to face me and offered his hand. "You will be a great leader for your people. I wish you all the best in your future endeavors and you have my promise as Lord Tang that no more of my kind will interlope on you or your kind's land."

"What is your kind?" I winched when Uncle Robert grunted. Wasn't sure if my question was rude or inappropriate. Either case, I'd asked.

"My people are not known to the world, but if we were . . . Most would consider us Vampires, but we are Blood Drinkers."

That explained . . . Teeth marks. Not fork. "You are serious."

"Young Theodor," Uncle Robert's short sharp tone told me more than the furious scowl I received. "Sorry, Commander Robert."

"He is fine, Commander Robert. He has the right to ask questions. He has to know all the facts if he is to be a leader."

"I will ensure he knows what is needed." Other words, Uncle Robert would inform me after he informed the other Royal Leaders. Uncle Robert waved at Uncle Alvin, who was stirring. "Help your Uncle into the house."

"Yes, Uncle Robert." I put my arm under Uncle Alvin's and lifted. Shock radiated through me as I helped Uncle Alvin inside.

Wasn't sure why shock had consumed me at that time, but I knew while I settled Uncle Alvin into a bed, fear crept back to life. I'd seen what the Blood Drinkers were able to do. Lots of damage and lots of blood. I might have been a future leader, but I'd still been a child.

Soon as Uncle Robert returned to check on Uncle Alvin, I threw my questions at him, but he told me he would fill me in after he spoke to the other Royal Leaders, but he never came back. Appeared he never told the others. Why? Had his cousins not given him time before they expelled him? The Awakening caused more trouble than three great leaders being kicked out of their seat of power and forced into hiding. Left all Royal Leaders further in the dark than they should have been. It'd taken me and my cousins eighty years to realize that the Awakening hadn't been the results of three Royal Leaders being killed. Nope. They'd thrown them into seclusion and exile. Secrets were truly the death of people.

Situations not attended to at the moment they arose led to upheaval. Left me with one option, whether I liked it or not. Next course of actions would not go over well with my cousins. Best if I handled things without their knowledge. Better to explain later than to ask permission. I hoped. My cousins seemed to disagree on most things.

I made my way down the steps and into the living room, where David, Caleb and Tray, David's Uncle, sat watching over Bryan and Larry.

Chapter 5

Theodor

"You two watch over Anthony and Franklin. I'll be gone for some time." A location for Lord Tang had to be discovered. Uncle Robert never told me where the attack happened, and Uncle Alvin never spoke of the incident to me again. Could not go to him since he had moved over to the Europe Bombardians. He disliked how we lived, so he changed venues.

"Why?" David asked.

"Got something to take care of."

"You do realize that - -"

"You two can handle things. If you need me, I'm a phone call away." I hoped my phone would work inside the Blood Drinker homeland. "If you need to take a vote you two know me well enough to know how I'd vote." David was the second to eldest Royal Leader and Caleb was the third eldest, we'd worked together eighty plus years. They knew me about as well as I knew myself.

I left them to unravel things for themselves. They'd get there at some point and time. If not . . . They would when I had the situation resolved. To do so meant . . . I needed answers and had someone at hand that hopefully could give me some.

"Tray," I waited until he looked at me. "Need to ask you a question."

"Sure."

"Hallway, please." Did not want Bryan and Larry to overhear. Bryan had enough on his plate and Larry, Anthony's Keeper, had just learned about Bombardians and Keepers and Protectors. Didn't need to be slammed with more.

"What's up?"

"Did Uncle Robert ever tell you guys about the creature that attacked Uncle Alvin?"

"You mean the one that happened the same day we were exiled?"

Yes. Uncle Robert had told the Royal Leaders. Why had the two who kicked Uncle Robert and the other two to the curb, not told the ones who replaced them or the ones who were in training to take their spots.

"Yes. What do you know about them?"

"The guy that came to aid your Uncle was the leader of the Blood Drinkers."

"So, they . . ." Even after hearing Lord Tang describe himself as a Vampire, I had never completely accepted the fact that someone drank blood to survive. Idea sickened me. "Are Vampires?" Seemed more proper to call them what they were. Vampires were folklore that drank blood, so if Lord Tang called themselves Blood Drinker then . . .

"They prefer Blood Drinkers. According to the guy they created the human stories of Vampires to keep themselves hidden. Unlike the stories, they don't feed on humans. They obtain their substance from other like them, or their fated partner."

"Then why . . . Attack Uncle Alvin?"

"Apparently, the Blood Drinker had gone rogue and decided to make life hard for Lord Tang."

What was I to say to that? We had our own rogues. Faced several of them only a few months ago.

"Was that all he told you?"

"All he knew."

"Did he tell you where the entrance to their land was?"

"Why you asking all this? Don't you already know it?"

"No."

"Was it not told to your dad?"

"If so . . . I was never told. Neither was the others." My beast roared and demanded answers, but there was no time to question my dad or the other ex-leaders. Up to me to find the answers and explain to the others.

"Robert told us the story and facts before we were exiled. In fact . . . He blames himself for us being exiled."

"Why? He did nothing wrong."

"I know that. He knows that, but he was the one that called the meeting to inform us of what happened to his brother. After they listened, they shifted the discussion to us and our Keepers being a disgrace."

"They were wrong."

"I know that, but you did not bring this topic up because of our dismissal."

"Right." I sighed. "We have received a message from Lord Tang."

"Ah . . . That's what took place upstairs when we arrived." Tray rested his back against the wall. "You going on your own to find him?"

I nodded.

"You not going to tell David and the others?"

"Not yet."

"Do you think it is wise to leave them in the dark?"

"Better to ask forgiveness than gain permission."

How come you never told them?"

"Thought they knew, plus I knew very little" Just that they existed, and they hid among Uncle Robert's lands. "Made a promise."

"You want me to keep my mouth shut about what you are up to?"

I nodded, taking in a deep breath, holding it.

"Don't like it, but I think David has enough to deal with."

"Thanks."

"The entrance was in the woods behind your Uncle's house. Apparently, Alvin strayed from his normal walking path and ran into an invisible wall in the farthest corner of Robert's land. As Alvin stepped back to try and find the barricade, he bumped into someone. The stranger attacked. Alvin stomped his foot and took off running."

Alvin had never been an excellent fighter. More of a coward than anything, which was what drove him to dislike our way of life. In

Europe there were less Mélange, so they did not need Bombardians with royal blood to be trackers. "Did Uncle Robert give you a sense of what he thought of them?"

"Dangerous. But he believed their leader would keep his word."

"Then why team up with our kind to deliver a message."

"No idea." Tray pushed off the wall, patting me on my shoulder. "I think you should at least tell them you know Lord Tang, but it's your decision."

Tray walked up the stairs, muttering about secrets being the death of people and that David had enough to handle. Tray had kept plenty of secrets through his life. That I was sure of. And he was right about David. Least I could do was put his mind at ease about any forthcoming attacks.

I followed Tray upstairs, catching a piece of a conversation between David, Caleb, and the other two.

"Truce? Why would they have kept that from us?" David shook his head. "Is this going to bring more danger to my home?"

"Doubt it." I topped the steps. "I know this one. Not sure what he wants, but I'm sure I can find out."

"Then this has nothing to do with me?" Anthony's eyes grew big as a plea shined from them.

"Lord Tang's interference don't, but Kevin may have chosen his own fate when he decided to turn on him." I squared my shoulders and shoved the tensing muscles to the back. "I'm going to be out of touch for awhile. David will be in charge of any situation that comes up. Take a vote if something arises that needs address before I get back."

"Hey," Anthony interjected before anyone else could. "You okay?"

Was. Wasn't. How could I be both? My cousins had known nothing about the Blood Drinkers existence, meaning no other royal blood carriers did either. Irked me. Then there was the fact that Lord Tang encroached on our kind after promising not to. My beast pushed for control so bad that my skin ached as it itched from the fur that was sprouting, thankfully, I wore a long sleeve shirt. Didn't need them to see me struggling to calm my beast. I'd been having trouble since Lord Tang showed up. Wasn't sure why. Didn't think my fear had been that bad. Maybe it had been. Only explanation I had. Wouldn't have been that bad if I had what David and Anthony had, a Keeper to calm my beast. Not a Protector. That would only make things worse. I had done my fair share of sleeping with women before David found his Keeper, but it had only been to try and create a child. I would not be doing that anymore. Two Royal Leaders found Keepers and fate would not stick me with a woman, a Protector. Nope. I had a Keeper out there somewhere and I would find him when the time was right.

"Will be."

Soon as all the secrets were revealed I could resume my search for my other half. If I wasn't meeting humans, I couldn't find the one that belonged to me. I, as much as any Bombaridan, needed my other half.

Chapter 6

Aidan

"I don't need you here, Aidan."

Lord Tang might not need me there, but I could not leave until I knew what his plan was. Lord Tang was an okay guy, but when things did not go his way, he became an ass. I'd been on the side of his temper more than once. I took it, even though I could have overcome his will. I never wanted to do that. Wasn't my life goal to lead a clan. I simply wanted to aid a leader and ensure the safety of the clan members. I was good at that.

"There is no need for you to wait for him to arrive."

"You sure he will come?" I wasn't. If I was him, I'd be pissed to high heaven, but . . . I'd also be sure to show a strong front. Question was, did he receive the right message from Lord Tang. It wasn't a clear one. Hardly one at all.

"He will come. He will not standby and allow me to invade a home like I did."

Lord Tang was right. No leader would do so, but would he come alone. Lord Tang had broken his word. He had interacted with the Bombardians after promising there'd be no contact between the two races.

"Would you not come?"

That's the problem. I would come and come in blazing. That's what put a bit of fear in me. How would Lord Tang react to such, if it took place.

"Go and make sure everything is running smooth."

"I'm sure everything is okay, or Rex would have contacted me."

"Don't care about what you think. I gave an order and expect it to be done without lip."

He'd get lip from me if something happened to my Inamorato. More than lip would take place.

"What is going to happen if he arrives?"

"We will talk."

"Talk?"

"Yes. I reached out to clear the situation up. He will do so."

"You sure he will?" Not sure I would have done anything Lord Tang requested of me after the stunt he pulled. Lord Tang might not have ordered that Kevin prick to invade the house, but he had them under his control. Or thought he had. It was rare for someone to slip the control of Lord Tang. Either he had not bound them to him tight enough, or they were stronger than he believed.

"He will come. Attempting to take a bite out of my hide, which he couldn't not do on his best day."

Lord Tang was more confident than I was. It did not take a mathematician to feel the power flow from their end of the hallway. No one would have been able to cut through it without an ice chipper or two. There were more than one streak of power coming from their end and each was as strong as the other one. Mix in the skillset and knowledge that their guards would have had . . . No way would our men and Lord Tang been able to take them down. Didn't matter how much Lord Tang believed he could eliminate them; he would not be able to. That was clearer than water.

"Then you need me here."

"No. That will only irritate him more. Best if I greet him alone."

Dang. I'd hoped to convince him to let me stay, but he would not give. Best I could do was watch from afar. Not what I wanted, but best I would get. Least if there was need of me, I'd be nearby.

Chapter 7

Theodor

Darn it. I shoved another large blade of grass from my face. No one had taken care of Uncle Robert's land since mom and dad moved to the mansion some forty years ago. Looked like a jungle. It'd taken me fifteen minutes to push aside all the waist high blade grass that reached for me and those that clung to my jeans as I trekked my way through the foliage to the entrance of the forest. I prayed it was still visible. Nature had a way of reclaiming what was hers. Really had no reason to worry. My memory was clear of the land's layout. I would never forget the section of forest that Uncle Robert and Lord Tang exited that day. We only met the once and it was the day I received notice that Uncle Robert had been killed. I assumed Lord Tang had hunted him down and killed him. I should have traced Uncle Robert's steps and sought out the Blood Drinker, but I'd been young and not strong enough to take down a grown man. As time went on, I let the fact Blood Drinkers might have killed him slip to the back of my mind. Life had been crazy after Uncle Robert's death. Dad had taken over the Royal Leader spot until I was old enough to step in. None of that should have kept me from speaking up about what happened and my thought of who killed Uncle Robert. But it did.

With caution I entered the woods and took the overgrown trail that Uncle Alvin took daily back then. Took me about an hour of walking to get to the spot Tray said the attack occurred. With tentative ease I lifted my hand, searching for any barriers. A bit too focused on locating the invisible wall led to me being caught by surprise by a large stump. I stumbled forward sticking my foot in it. Literally.

One foot slipped into a hole, but it was like I was in two different zones. Realms. Something like that. One side of my body was surrounded by a thick, vibrate trees while the other was in what resembled a dead zone. No life. Dull green foliage closed in around me while the other side was full of color and life. Was as if Earth existed, but not at the same time.

"You looking for me?"

I spun in a circle until the sun flickered off a smooth surface. There appeared to be two men standing in the shadow, but I wasn't sure. "Lord Tang?"

"One and only?"

He deserved a roll of the eyes, but his at ease tone sickened me. Him and his goons had barged into David's home. Turned Bombardians on their own kind in order to do his dirty work. None of which went along with the promise he'd made. My people had done so. How could they not. None knew about his kind except me.

"Guess you are confused."

"Confused?" Boy was I. Irked. Ticked. Pissed. Explained it better than confused. My beast pushed for control. Hard. Was all I could do to keep him in the background. I was ticked, and so was my beast, but not to the point that it would all but rend me in half. What was going on? Was my beast becoming unhinged because it had no one to calm it? Was that even possible? Never heard of such, but . . . Never heard of a Royal Leader having a Keeper until a few months ago. What else lurked underneath us that we were not aware of?

"They weren't exactly your kind."

"What!" Lord Tang's smartass attitude was not helping me control my beast, but I had no other option, so I threw a mental chain around the mental cage I barricaded my beast inside when he acted up.

"They were . . . Sick."

"They were well until . . ."

"Sick in the mind, or I would not have been able to control their bodies."

"They were not sick. They turned Mélange." I pointed a finger at him. "Still my kind."

"No." Lord Tang crossed his arms. "They renounced the Royal Leaders. Openly. Told me they did not follow you."

Course they did. They were twisted Bombaridans. They'd lost their other half. Didn't mean they weren't part of my people. "You are splitting hairs."

"Whatever you say." Lord Tang pulled a sheet of paper from his pocket. "I had a reason for reaching out."

"I assumed you did, but you could have done so with a bit more taste and less fire."

"Might could have, but . . . I'm old. Like to have fun once in a while."

"Games?" Who the hell did the man think he was? God or something. "I'm not one for games. More of the upfront kind of guy. So are my cousins."

"Fine. I'll make amends later." Lord Tang held out the sheet of paper. "I have a . . . He is . . . He's under my protection and has been for eighteen years. The other day . . ." Lord Tang waved the paper. "Take a look and see what appeared on his arm."

I glanced at the sheet of paper, knowing instantly what I saw. Clear as day. A Marked One. The mark of a Keeper. Whoever the arm belonged to had been marked by his Bombardian. His forearm was no longer bare. A tattoo of a sidewards W with the word Bombardian Keeper. Once the Keeper made his decision the name of his Bombardian would appear as well. The owner of the forearm was a beast calmer. Was in for a life of happiness and wholeness if he chose his Bombardian. Bombardians and Keepers fell in love ninety percent of the time. Lived a long life at each other's side. How could they not, the human held the Bombardians life in his palm.

"See you know what this is."

"Do."

"What am I to do about it?"

"Nothing."

"He's under my protection."

"May be, but he's a Keeper."

"A what?"

"He's the one person who can calm the inner beast of a the Bombardian he belongs to."

"He belongs to me."

"That is up to him and his Bombardian."

"No."

"Afraid you have no say. It is between him and his Bombardian." I handed Lord Tang the photo back. "This is why you sent goons into my cousin's house?"

"I did not send them anywhere."

"Did you not recruit these Bombardians?"

"Yes, but . . . I did not give them the order to invade your cousin's house."

"No, you put Kevin, who had an agenda of his own, in charge."

"Unfortunate mistake on my part." Lord Tang huffed. "Still, I knew no other way to contact you."

"Ever thought of a phone call."

"Not like you are listed in the phone book."

"I am."

"Uh . . . What?" Lord Tang stood up taller. "You are serious."

"I have a number listed. I have an appearance to uphold."

"Well . . . Damn."

"Yeah. Now I have a pissed off cousin. Four actually, because if you mess with one, you mess with us all."

"I . . . Shit. This sucks ass." Lord Tang's shoulders slumped. "I fucking hate apologizing." He muttered.

"Don't we all."

"Good, then this is over with."

"You call that an apology?"

"Best you going to get." Lord Tang slid down the tree he leaned against. "What do I do about my friend?"

"Does he know who put the mark on him?"

Lord Tang shook his head.

"No one new has approached him."

"No. Told you he was under my protection. Has been since he was a babe."

"Who new has come into his life."

"No one."

"Someone must have."

"Why you say that?"

"There is only one way a Bombardian can know to cast the spell that marks their Keeper or Protector."

"How?"

"They come into contact or catch a hint of their scent." I sat on the ground across from him. "Once the spell is cast the Bombardian will make face-to-face contact."

"No one can do such."

"Why do you say that?"

"My friend does not leave my home."

Why would someone not go outside. Even the . . . "He is an Agoraphobia?"

"No. He's under my protection."

"You keep saying that." I threw my hands in the air. "What does that mean?"

"I can not protect him if he is running about. I do not have the people to escort him everywhere he might go, so he does not leave the sanctity of the warded area. And I can promise you no one has entered my domain since your Uncle Alvin. If what you say is true, then how did this mark appear on my friend's arm."

No clue. Not something I'd heard of. It would take some research.

"Why are you scratching your head?"

"Never heard of such."

"Such?"

"The mark can only come about by a Bombaridan casting a spell." Wasn't about to tell the Blood Drinker more than that. No need for him to know the spell required a name, or that the Marked One had to be a certain age. Ah . . . The young man had recently turned eighteen. Or . . . The Bombardian had not seen him since he had. Was that possible?

"You are leaving something out." Lord Tang hissed.

"Did you hiss?"

"Yes."

"Why?"

"It does not bother you?"

"Why should it?" Not like a hiss could harm me. I'd faced worse when I went face to face with a Mélange. Those were some mean bastards when riled up.

"It does most people."

"Bombardians are not most people."

"Right. Wolf inside."

"Yes." One thing. "Did you expect me to tell you secrets of my race?"

"I expected the truth."

Stupid. "You have it."

"I got only more questions."

Answers I would have to find out on my own. There was no way I could involve my cousins in this mess. They knew the danger was over and David had his hands full with his pregnant Keeper. Not to mention Anthony had just sealed himself to his Keeper, meaning the two would pretty much hump like bunnies for a few months. That meant Caleb and Franklin needed their full focus to help David and Anthony keep their Royal Keepers happy. Then there was handling the fact that Larry was the president of the United States son. We were going to be working out a way to bring the Bombardians to the world. Or so I hoped. We'd tried to find a way to do so for twenty-one years. Once that was done, things would go into an uproar. Nope. My cousins did not need me bothering them with having to figure out how a Keeper was marked when he had not been around a Bombardian.

Chapter 8

Aidan

Sexy oozed from my other half as his body swayed with each step. With a straight back, emphasizing his already impressive height, his shoulders appeared broader than life itself. Long dark hair hung loosely around his face, drawing my eyes to his sexy triangle shaped slanted eyes. Most would have thought him walking in his sleep, but I knew better. Those enamoring eyes took in every aspect of the land and outer edges. I knew he would be astute, which was why I'd taken residence further back than most would have. My scent might blow his way, but I bet he would be more focused on what was taking place closer to him than off in a distance. Not to mention I had no idea if my scent would call to him. Most Inamorato felt the pull upon sight, not scent. Then again . . . What little time I had to inquire about the situation I faced came back with what I expected. No one knew about another race; therefore it had never been heard of. My father had been very interested in the fact that I knew of a different race when he did not and should have. He questioned me intensely about when, where, how, and what I knew about them. He had all but busted my eardrums when I told him that Lord Tang had ran across them several decades ago. Lord Tang would have to answer to my dad about that. I was just glad it was not my responsibility to report such information to the Hierarchy Clanman.

None of that mattered to me, but it had taken me answering those questions before I could get my own questions answered. Not that I got any. Did get permission to do what had to be done to claim my Inamorato. The Hierarchy Clanman told me that no Blood Drinker could be told to forgo an Inamorato for any reason, including race, sex, and species. That put my racing mind at ease. Still, I did not want to announce who the Bombardian Leader was until I knew more about him. Name would be the most helpful. I would not gain much from watching him interact with Lord Tang. My reason for spying, and disobeying my Lord, was to ensure the safety of my Inamorato. My other half came here at the behest of my Lord and did not deserve to be disrespected or harmed. I'd make sure neither happened.

I listened and gaged each move and eye motion that the leader made. Tension clung to his bulky muscles as he slid down the tree. He appeared at ease, but it did not take a genius to realize he was on high alert. He spoke calmly and respectfully, but tightness clung to every word. Not that it shouldn't had. If I had been him I, would have been tearing into Lord Tang. I had tried to tell Lord Tang there was a less domineering method to contact the Bombardian leader, but he'd been adamant that there was none. Guess he knew how wrong he was.

The moment the Bombardian leader saw the photo of Connor's arm I knew he knew what was going on. As the conversation went on, I learned quite a bit. Nothing that helped me discover a way to announce to the leader that he belonged to me. Nor did I gain a better knowledge of what a Marked One was, beside the . . .

Crap. I had learned more than I expected, also gave me more questions. How did I find out the answers? I could not walk up to the Bombardian leader and ask him. Lord Tang would rip me in half. Or try. Did not need a war to start over a rash reaction. Nope. I had to go about this the right way. How was that though? How did I find out more about these Keepers? What they were, beside a beast calmer? What kind of beast? What did *belong to* mean? Did everyone Bombardian have one of these Keepers?

Loads of question invaded my thoughts, making me unable to concentrate, making me miss the rest of Lord Tang's conversation. Darn it. I needed to hear it. There would have been much more information for me. I was sure of it. Just . . .

Come on Lord Tang, for once in your life be confused and ask for him to explain again. One thing the Lord Tang believed in was being clear on every subject, even if he had to have it repeated five times. I just needed him to be that way this time.

I waited and waited while Lord Tang and the Bombardian leader discussed how to handle the situation. To me, it appeared that there was nothing that Lord Tang could do. From what I gaged it was in the hands of the Bombardian that Connor belonged to. Whatever that meant. Lord Tang would not go for such. Lord Tang had taken care of Connor since he was born. He would not allow someone to come in and take him from him. Nope. There would be . . . Darn it. Lord Tang would start a war over Connor. My dad would shit a brick. Not to mention the Hierarchy Clanman would rip him into shreds and piss on him. Lord Tang was in enough trouble with our head leader. Much more from Lord Tang and he might lose his Clan Leader position.

Oh crap! I winched as Lord Tang's voice boomed through the area. I looked behind me to ensure that no one was nearby. We did not need the guards charging to the rescue when there was no threat. That would only cause an issue. Lord Tang would think they were in one, even though the proposition made sense.

Chapter 9

Theodor

"You want to what!"

Shouting? What was up with that? Request wasn't unreasonable. Lord Tang requested assistance in understanding what had taken place inside his domain. Was his charge that had become a Marked One. To unwind how that happened questions had to be asked. Had to discover who around him was . . .

"Are all the people around him Blood Drinkers?"

Lord Tang halted his pacing and lifted an eyebrow.

"Well?"

"All but two. I know they are human. I would have picked up on your . . . Unusual odor."

What the . . . Did he say I stunk?

"Don't get offensive." Lord Tang held his hands up. "It's just that your Uncles, and you bare a . . . You hold a stronger scent of - -"

"You seriously saying we stink?"

"No. Lord no. It is more of a chocolate, vanilla scent. Kind of . . . Enticing."

What the hell? He switched to saying he was attracted to me. Not that it bothered me. Lord Tang was a handsome man. Long black hair encircled his long slender jaw line, just like I loved. His tall, semi-muscled body fit the kind of men I brought home.

I shook my head, shoving the thoughts aside, because all it was doing was make my cock hard. I'd been that way since I arrived. Not to mention my wolf was shoving for control. Neither of those actions were common for me. I did not mix pleasure with business, nor did I need to mix it up with another race. I was here for one purpose. That's what mattered and I had done what was best for my people. I'd give my help, ensure that the Marked One was okay and had spoken to his Bombardian and then I'd get back to my cousins and everyday life. My help would be required since our entire world was about to go to the crazy side for some time. Alerting the world to what we are will cause a bigger uproar than when the Destroyer's Hermitages were created.

"Let's get back on track." I stood. "You reached out for my help. I can't do that unless I see the gentleman in question and the ones who interact with him."

"I . . . This isn't . . . I promised his parents . . ."

"What is so special about this young man?"

"I can't - -"

"Listen, you wanted my help. I have to know all the facts to seek out the right people to uncover how this young man became marked if no Bombardian has been around him."

Lord Tang's fingertips dug into the bark of the tree he stood beside. David would have thrown the man fifty yards for doing such. David despised anyone to disturb Earth out of frustration and anger. He swore his affinity gave no aid to those who harmed her. I would not dispute him. I knew Fire would refuse aid if I went to it with death or revenge in my mind. Unless . . . It was to condemn someone who harmed one of its own.

A piece of bark peeled away as Lord Tang ripped his fingers free. He resumed his pacing, throwing patches of grass from his heels. Didn't know the man well, but I was sure he debated how to handle the situation. I felt sorry for him. I understood promises and responsibilities, but I also knew they made life difficult and brought trouble. Lately, there'd been lots of them coming at me and my cousins. Each one had been more difficult to handle, but the last one brought a nice little gift. One Bombardians had been longing for. I wasn't sure if the spot I found myself in would turn out good. One thing was clear, I'd have to reach out to Uncle Robert and the other two exiled Royal Leaders. Might even have to involve David's father.

"Okay." Lord Tang stopped in front of me. "There are some restrictions for entering my domain." I'd like to say the man spoke to me. He basically hissed and it was more like a garbled-up mess that I caught the meaning of. "Do not lift an eyebrow at me."

Had I? Most likely. My beast disliked being ordered when trying to help. I wasn't keen on it but could hand it. I hoped. Really depended on what the restrictions were.

"One . . ." Lord Tang lifted a finger in my face, drawing a deep rumble from me. "You can not bring anyone with you. No matter what. Two . . ." Another finger went up. "You will not be able to leave until the situation is resolved. Three . . ." His third finger lifted forcing me to smack his hand out of my face. He ignored it. "You will never speak of the man you meet, or anyone else in my domain."

"No." I spun and made two steps toward the invisible barrier before he grabbed my arm. "Let me go. Now."

He released me but moved in front of me. "You have to understand where I am coming from. I can not allow our existence to come to life. I have people to answer to as well."

Understandable, but . . . "I can not agree to those and help you."

"Why not?"

I heaved and stretched my neck left then right. "I may have to reach out to others. If I can't leave . . ." No sense in speaking the obvious. Lord Tang's head moved back and forth like a swing. Lack of comprehension was astounding. Bit aggravating as well. He'd came to me in the most disrespectful manner. No retaliation came his way. I came to see the asswipe. Agreed to help him, even though he'd caused chaos in David's house while he was gone.

"You have to understand - -"

"I do not have to do anything." I snarled. "All I have to do is be the Royal Leader of the Bombardians. You have done nothing but disrespect us from the moment you sent thug Bombardians after Commander Anthony and invaded Commander David's home."

"That was not my - -"

"Do not go there. They worked for you. Therefore, you are responsible for their actions." My beast roared for respect and retribution.

"Fine." Lord Tang held his hands up and took a step back. "I am . . . I did not mean to disrespect you."

"You can not even apologize, and you wish me to agree to ridiculous restrictions while I help solve a problem . . ." I was a breath away from telling him he caused the problem and that it did not concern me, but . . . It wasn't the truth. A Bombardian had marked a human. If the Bombardian did not get to see his Keeper, then he would become Mélange. There were enough of them running around. Did not wish more of my kind to become half wolf, half human. I wanted everyone of them to find the one that calms their beast and makes them happy for the rest of their lives. "I want to help. Not for you, but my Bombardian."

"Then why not agree to my limitations?"

"I have never heard of a mark coming up without the spell being cast. If there is no Bombardian around your young charge then I will have to reach out to some ex-Royal Leaders. If they have not heard of such then I will have to do some research that will bring in my cousins."

"I can't . . . Damn it." Lord Tang sighed. "Fine. Fine. You can come in and meet each of the clan members and the other humans that work for me. We can approach the other issues if they arise."

"That is doable." The roaring inside my head intensified. Why? He had gotten Lord Tang to agree. What was up with him giving me such a hard time? Didn't matter. I had a job to finish. "Lead the way."

Chapter 10

Theodor

I might have made a deal with the devil, but . . . No other choice came to mind. Not to mention my curiosity was as high as my need to aid the Bombardian and his Keeper. It was that had my feet moving on their own accord as soon as I had an agreement with Lord Tang.

Bright green grass greeted me as we walked further into the domain. Earth surely had been gracious to Lord Tang and his area. Bright green leaves filled dark rich branches and buds bloomed from every flower in sight. Lord Tang might have gone about things the wrong way, but he had the love of Earth and a place David would be at peace in. Or he might have if Lord Tang had not invaded his house. Even though I despised Lord Tang's actions, I understood the hardships that arose from being a leader of a hidden race. For over a century Bombardians struggled to coincide alongside humans, even after the President created the Cult and its leader, the Red Hooded Guy. As if that wasn't bad enough, the President turned the Red Hooded Guy into some kind of boogieman to keep children in-line. President went further making them fear the mark and the Destroyer's Hermitages, the homes for those who bore their Bombardians mark but chose to live apart from them, seeing them every other day. Such action allowed the Bombardian to control their beast.

Hadn't been our best solution, least it kept many Bombardians from turning into a Mélange. Even after all that, former and current Royal leaders never felt it necessary to hide our people away from the entire world. It made no sense to seclude oneself. It limited a person's entire life. It also drove some mad. If we'd done that, all Bombardians might have been stuck in half state the rest of their lives.

"While you are here," Lord Tang came to stop in front of a light brown cabin with a huge front porch baring a white swing. "You will stay here. It has all the necessities you need. All I ask is that you do not wander around without me, or one that I appoint to escort you. This isn't to restrict your movement, but to ensure your safety. I have never allowed anyone, other than those who swore loyalty to me, to enter the domain. I am not sure how my people will react."

Sounded overboard, but . . . Who was I to second guess how one operated their area? "How long have you and your clan lived here?"

"Way longer than you have been alive."

Damn. I'd lived almost a century, eighty plus of those as Royal Leader. Training for the position had begun soon as I was able to talk.

"Who do you see first?"

Right. What would benefit me? The humans around the guy or the guy himself. It would be nice to know who I was trying to help. It wasn't my place to explain all the details to the guy. That belonged to his Bombardian and I would not take such a special moment from one of mine.

"Introduce me to the Marked One."

"Why do you call them that?"

"It is the name we adopted from the humans. Most of our kind refer to them as Keeper for the men and Protector for the women."

"Well his name is Connor O'Brien."

"Irish?"

"Yes."

"How long has he been under your protection?"

"Eighteen years."

"Since he was a baby?"

"Since he was born."

He was a youngster. One who would have just came into his Keeper age. It explained why there was no connection made between his Bombardian and Keeper earlier.

"What happened to his parents?"

"His father was killed during a battle between my clan and a neighboring one. His wife was three months along."

"And his mother?"

"Died during childbirth."

"That's why you put him under your protection."

"Sort of."

"What does that mean?" I stopped and crossed my arms the moment I saw Lord Tang's eye go blank.

"Why do you need to know this?"

"More I know . . . Better I can judge the entire situations." Was the truth, but the story intrigued me. I could not see Lord Tang giving just anyone his protection. Man was a huge prick and thought himself God. That's how I read his actions as of late.

"The O'Brien family has been with my clan for generations. Connor is the last living one."

"Then his family line ends with him."

"Not if I have my way."

Oh boy! No way to keep that from happening. Man was a Keeper. That meant he would end up with his Bombardian, either by his side or living in a Destroyer's Hermitage, or have his memory erased and be relocated. Law stated those who chose to see their Bombardian every other day or two had to live in one of the homes. Until the entire situation was worked out with the President that was the law.

"I know what you are thinking and it is not going to happen." Lord Tang resumed walking. "Connor does not live among the humans, therefore their laws does not concern him."

"And if he makes a contract with his Bombardian?"

"Will not happen."

"You have no say in that."

"I do." Lord Tang came to stop in front of a red house with blue windows. On the porch sat a young, sandy brown haired man. He casually rocked as he smiled down at us. "Connor."

"Lord Tang." Connor nodded to Lord Tang, but shifted his eyes to me, giving me a small tilt of the head. "Who do we have here?"

"Connor, do you care if we join you for awhile?"

"Sure. There are more chairs in the corner."

Lord Tang moved up the stairs and appeared to float over to the chairs, removing two and sitting them against the railing. "How is your day going?"

"It has been fine. I hope it remains that way."

Man was smart. Knew when to be suspicious and how to play the unexpected off. Made a great fit for a Bombardian.

"I have finally heard from the gentleman I told you could clear up the mark." Lord Tang motioned for me to take a seat. "This is Commander Theodor."

"Nice to meet you."

Connor held his hand out to me. I made sure to give him my best smile as I shook his hand. "Same. May I ask you a few questions."

"If Lord Tang agrees."

"It is fine." Lord Tank kicked his legs out, letting himself rest against the side of Connor's rocker.

"Then ask away."

Man was good. Did not take long to pick up on the fact that Connor was way smarter than I'd expected. He knew how to play to Lord Tang. How to make him think he had the upper hand, when he did not. It would not shock me if the young man knew all about Bombardians and what he was. Gave me the perfect plan of attack.

"Do you remember what you were doing when the mark appeared?"

"Taking a walk."

"Inside Lord Tang's domain?"

"Where else would he walk." Lord Tang hissed.

Seemed to be lots of places for Connor to stray if he desired to. Bryan, David's Keeper and Tommy, General Cain's Keeper always found ways to see one another when Bryan's parents forbid him from seeing Tommy.

"Lord Tang," I glanced his way, "I have to have the correct information to understand the entire situation." My beast snarled and cursed Lord Tang's tight and stiff body. Might have been best if I had asked to speak to Connor alone. If Connor had found a way out of Lord Tang's domain he would not admit it in front of Lord Tang.

"I was on the outskirts and Ronnie was with me. Like always during the day."

"Is he human?" I kept my eye on Connor, but it was more than clear that my question was directed at Lord Tang.

"Yes."

"How long has he worked for you?"

"Thirty-five years."

Long time. Long enough that Lord Tang would have picked up on any differences. It wouldn't have been hard for a Bombardian to keep himself hidden unless . . . Bombardian's over one hundred found it harder to control their beast.

"He does not have your identifying scent."

Didn't mean much. I'd never heard of any of my kind bearing such. But I'd not been around Blood Drinkers.

"What do you mean, Lord Tang?"

Lord Tang informed Connor of what he believed to be facts. Until I heard it from other Blood Drinkers then I did not find it credible. Might not even then. Yet . . . Who knew.

"Do you recall . . ." I turned when a step squeaked. It was the most wonderful moment of my life and explained a few things.

Chapter 11

Aidan

My cock had been hard since my other half had entered the domain. Drove me crazy to sit back and watch him interact with Lord Tang, but I knew it had to be done. I gotten the information from my leaders, but I needed to know more about him. How to approach him. What he was? And my gut told me that whatever was going on with Connor would assist me as well. My plan had been to be tag along from a distance as Lord Tang took my other half around, but Lord Tang changed all that when he put the command the Clan in my hands. Spoke of my loyalty greatly, but that wasn't new to me. I'd been Lord Tang's second in command for over one hundred years. I was about the only one who would put up with his excessive controlling manners. Most of the Clan tolerated his ways because he was the only Lord that did not adhere to the extreme old ways. I just hoped he kept that attitude when he found out about my Inamorato.

Lord Tang had been on the edge of an explosion since Connor's mark appeared. Not that I could blame him. Somehow someone got close enough to Connor to apply another race's mark. Not that . . . Okay, Connor was another race and Lord Tang knew that. Still he had raised him. Raised him might not have been the best choice of words. More like kept him from everything human related. Connor knew the ins and outs of the Blood Drinkers way of life but had only met a handful of humans and all of those had sworn loyalty to Lord Tang. Doing so they sold their souls to him. If they displeased him or disrespected him their lives came to an abrupt end. Thankfully, only one had met that fate.

None of that mattered to me. All I wanted was to sink my cock into the hot man that had entered my homelands. I knew I could not keep him here. Wasn't stupid. He was a leader of his kind. He had a predetermined life and job. Question was . . . How did I fit into that?

What would happen when I told him he was my other half. The one I was to spend the rest of my life with. What would Lord Tang say? Least I knew that it did not matter to the ones that oversaw the entire Blood Drinker race. What I feared most was that the Hierarchy would reach out to Lord Tang about the Bombardian race before I spoke to my Inamorato or Lord Tang. Then again . . . I've known Lord Tang to ignore his phone for over a month before. Would work in my favor if he did so again.

My keys clinked as my phone vibrated. One look told me I was not going to be happy. "What's up, Ralph?"

"I can't make my shift. Can you cover for me?"

"What is the issue this time?"

Ralph and his Inamorato had been having difficulties. Ralph longed for them to have a wee-one, but his Inamorato was very young and thought they had a long life, meaning more than enough time to build a family. She wanted him to build a nice nest egg before they had children. Ralph was trying to show her that money wasn't an issue in our clan. We all helped each other out. One of the ways he'd been going about it was to avoid work when they had an argument. Lord Tang knew what was taking place. Agreed with his action but told him he would only let it go so far. Since there was an unknown among them . . . Lord Tang . . .

"She's late."

"Late?"

"Ugh . . ." Ralph's words dropped low. "Her cycle is four days late."

Cyc - - Ah shit. "You smell anything different?"

"She bears two odors, other than hers."

Shit. "Twins?"

"Sure of it."

"Has she picked up on it?"

"Says no, but . . ."

He didn't believe her. "She outright lie?"

"Not outright." Ralph sighed. "Okay, she did. Wasn't hard to miss the rotten piss flowing from her when I asked."

"Why do you think she lied?" Lying to your Inamorato was a big no-no. Other Blood Drinkers could not detect lies, but an Inamorato knew their other halves scent like their next breath and certain odors told stories. Just like I knew my Inamorato belonged to me by the potent scent of chocolate and vanilla cream. First whiff of that glorious aroma sent me into another frame of mind. That amazing smell was why I'd been hard for the last few hours.

"She's not happy . . ."

Why would any woman not be? A wee-one was a blessing. It kept their family line alive and gave them a deep connection with someone she brought life to and could nurture. My mom always fussed at me because I knew at a young age that my Inamorato would be a man. She told me I was wrong for the longest time, but before she passed on, she told me she hoped I found the other half I deserved. And that I deserved a man that would love me with all their heart. My dad had not agreed with her, but he did not seem distraught over my Inamorato being of another race. Not that I told him it was a man. Or had I? I might have. Oh well.

". . . I was just given a very young Inamorato and one that came from a poor Clan."

"Do you regret me sending you on that assignment?"

"No, Aidan. Not for one second. I love my woman; she's just not adjusting to our way of life as fast as I expected. I thought it would be amazing thing for her to be a part of a financially stable clan."

I'd feared that would be an issue when Ralph came home with her. He had been adamant that a couple of months living among our clan would show her that life was a hundred times better than where she grew up.

“I think,” Ralph’s tone livened up, “her carrying our children will show her that we are not like her old clan. That our clan works as a whole and has money to take care of each other.”

“Hope so.” I glanced at the clock. “I’ll cover for you.” Would get me close to my Inamorato. For some time. Wasn’t sure what Lord Tang and our guest decided, but I knew he was in our domain. If I was out and about, I might run into him. Get a better look, give him time to take note of me. Only way he would discover our connection. “Good luck with your Inamorato and congrats on your upcoming wee-ones.”

Chapter 12

Theodor

Had to uncross my legs and shift my position among the wooden folding chair. Blueberries and vanilla consumed my nose, reminding me of my mother's cobbler. Every holiday that rolled around it greeted our entire family.

"Sir."

Butter would have melted at the steady, firm, yet soft voice. With ease I slid my eyes over every inch of the tall drink of water standing in front of Lord Tang. Each inch or two was another wonderful masculine aspect of perfection. Newcomer had perfect firm legs and arms. Broad chest that I'd love to lick. A face that had the right amount of puffy cheeks and rounded eyes that accentuated his light red pupils surrounded by midnight blue eyes. Short cut hair allowed me to see a cute little button style nose. Not a man I would have taken home to fuck on any other day, but . . .

"Uh . . . Commander Theodor?"

Who was . . . Shit. A shake of my head lessened the lust, but my eyes remained on the newcomer.

"Yes, Lord Tang."

"Uh . . . You do know that we can smell as well as your kind."

Fuck. Well . . . He knew how I felt about the man. Did the newcomer? Was he a Blood Drinker? Who was the one that drove my beast wild with lust and had it squirming under my skin? My beast demanded I throw the man against the wall and thrust into him hard and all at once. Claiming him in the most primal manner. More than that, my beast and human side, longed to cast the spell that would mark the god-looking gentlemen as mine. Couldn't do that. Not until . . .

"Aidan," Lord Tang's voice was rough and held a bit of sharpness that threw my beast into an uproar. Lord Tang was . . . Not upset, but my beast despised him talking to its Keeper.

KEEPER! I had one. Thank goodness. One of my biggest fears had been receiving a Protector. It'd died down a bit after David found his. Even more when Anthony found Larry. Led me to the conclusion that all five Royal Leaders would have Keepers. Discovering that a Royal Keeper could produce children put my mind at further ease. An . . . Unbelievable thing, but an amazing discovery.

"Yes, Lord Tang."

My eyes met his red ones, sighing deeply. Aidan. What a wonderful, sexy, and fitting name. How could light blue sparkles light up the man's eyes as he met mine. Aidan's full attention was on me, just like it should be the rest of my life.

"What are you doing here?"

Aidan's chest lifted and fell as his eyes darted to Lord Tang but came right back to mine. "I . . . I . . . I . . . Ralph was unable to keep his shift. I'm filling in."

"Again?"

Their conversation continued, but Aidan's attention remained on me. Mine was on his bobbing Adam-apple.

"Yes, Lord Tang. I will let him fill you in."

Bing . . . Bing . . . Bing . . .

What in the world. Each time the sound echoed through the air my ears twinged. Aggravated me, but not enough I let my eyes search out the source.

I had a Keeper. The mere thought was hard to swallow. Not in a bad way. In an amazing, great, wonderful manner. More like a dream come true.

"Aidan, listen to me."

The sharp commanding tone ripped a low snarl from me. I sprang out of my chair, blocking Lord tang's line of sight. My chest ached from the intense growl rippling from it.

Lord Tang flew from his seat, hissing, giving a snarl of his own. He said something, but I could not understand him thanks to his fangs.

It was those that managed to allow me to regain control of my beast. Didn't mean I was pleased Lord Tang gave my Keeper such disrespect, but Aidan and Lord Tang had no clue what had changed. Could not until I cast the spell. Then again . . .

Damn. Fuck. Another against the grain pairing. Was a Royal Leader never going to find a Keeper or Protector that was normal?

How had I been giving a Blood Drinker as a Keeper? Was Aidan a Blood Drinker?

"Introduce us." I stepped back.

"No." Lord Tang's fang retracted, but his face appeared to be on fire, matching his red-orange shirt.

"Yes."

"No. He has nothing to do with the situation you are here to handle."

Lord Tang was . . . Not completely correct. Aidan might not have a direct connection to Connor, but he would soon bare his own mark. But . . .

"Aidan," Lord Tang waved at the house. "Until I leave you are not needed. Wait inside."

Take a flying leap was a second from leaving my mouth when my mind caught up. Such a response would do nothing but cause an uproar. Took all my willpower not to demand Aidan remain at my side. A voice of reason told me to handle things with kid gloves or face a full-on battle between my kind and the Blood Drinkers. Until I knew more . . . Could not risk such until I knew their strengths and weakness. Crash course on Blood Drinkers was required. Where would it come from?

"Yes, Lord Tang." Aidan nodded at me, smiling before he lowered his head and went inside.

"Care to explain what is going on between you and my subject?"

"Not right now." Time to come to terms with what Aidan being my Keeper meant. Doing so without alerting Lord Tang was best. Might not happen. Right then I had to get to the bottom of Connor's Bombardian. "Connor, do you recall who was around when the mark appeared?"

"My guard and a friend."

Vague. Spoke loudly but got me no closer to an answer.

"Which one?" Lord Tang leaned back, but kept his eyes locked on me. The beast snorted and snarled, making my skin crawl and itch. Lord Tang's action made sense. Poor reaction towards a subject . . .

Aidan was a Blood Drinker. Every time Lord Tang spoke of a human, he addressed them as such, not subject. He reserved that title for his Blood Drinkers. My interference with Lord Tang and Aidan set him off. Someone doing such to me would have ended up a hundred yards away in one swift toss. Had to be taking all Lord Tang's control not to be up in my face. Showed strength and respect.

"Daniel and Kyle were the guards." Connor picked at his fingernails. "Robin was with us."

"Robin?" Lord Tang sat forward, frowning which made Connor push back into the swing.

Fear? Unease? Tension? All the above. Just what I needed.

"I thought I told you to stop hanging around him."

Interesting. What bothered Lord Tang about them two being friends?

"I know, but . . ."

"There is no but. You and him, know what I said."

"Yes, but . . ."

"There is no but. You both broke my rule."

"Not really."

"What!"

Lord Tang was all but out of his seat. Connor's hands were pickle beat red from squeezing the edge of the swing. His tone screamed hesitation, but determination.

"You told us not to be alone. The guards were there."

"That's splitting hairs. You know him and you left the area the last time. I can not have such actions from you or any of my workers. It is not safe for you or anyone under my rule."

Worker, not . . . Shit. "Uh . . . Lord Tang, thought you said he'd not been outside your confines."

"I forgot he took a small trip."

"Did he run across anyone during his expedition?"

Connor was behaving like . . . A young man who'd been kept hidden. Forbidden to stretch his independence. Searching out contact from his own kind. For the most part. Connor had been kept from basic understanding and interaction with people like him.

"Did you?" Lord Tang sat back.

"No. We were only picking the berries I wanted."

"How long was you out there?" Only took two seconds to run across someone. Bombardians were known for taking hikes to calm themselves. When Connor's face dipped further, I knew Lord Tang would despise his answer.

"Twenty minutes."

"It did not take you that long to pick a few berries. What else were you two up to?" Lord Tang snapped, making Connor jerk back.

My beast shoved at my confines. It was fed-up with Lord Tang's disrespect. And that was all it was. Connor might be under Lord Tang's protection, but he was a Keeper, making him one of my people, just like Aidan would be.

More hissing had Connor pulling his legs up to his chest. I hadn't meant to get the young man in trouble, but . . .

His Bombardian would feel his Keeper's distress and come running if it became deep enough.

"It is . . . We . . . I . . . Him and I . . ."

Rich green smoke formed around Connor, driving Lord Tang to his feet.

Chapter 13

Theodor

Not the wisest . . . A seven-foot, broad shoulder, bald man appeared in front of Connor. Arms hung loosely and his eyes roamed the area, taking in the entire situation in one quick scan. Aidan rushed from the house as ten Blood Drinkers leapt over the porch banister. Connor sprang to his feet, shouting not to hurt him. Gave one of the Blood Drinkers the opportunity to snatch him from behind and rushed him to the middle of the group of Blood Drinkers. Lord Tang hissed worse than a snake ready to strike. The Bombardian growled as his nose and jaw began to realign.

I was the only sane person. I cupped my hands around my mouth and shouted.

"Hold it."

Didn't work, so I stuck two fingers in my mouth and whistled.

Blood Drinkers threw their hands over their ears. The Bombardian, who had completed his shift, dropped to his belly. Connor didn't seem bothered by it. He used the unexpected noise to shove his way through the group of protectors. He dropped to the wolf's side and threw himself over it. Keeper at his best. Whoever claimed Connor had gotten a good hearted and loyal man. Looked as if there'd be no new Mélange. Thank goodness.

"What in the . . ." Lord Tang earned a snarl and snap of my teeth when he shoved his chest into mine.

"It would be in your best interest," my teeth clanked after each word. I'd taken all the disrespect I could stand. "For you to back the fuck off me and get rid of your hoard of Blood Drinkers. Minus Aidan."

Why not kill two birds with one stone. While I let the Bombardian explain his marking of Connor, I'd let Aidan gain useful knowledge. Handy. From the way Aidan shot out of the house he'd heard Lord

Tang hissing, meaning he was devoted to Lord Tang. Good for Lord Tang. Bad for me.

"Best check your attitude." Lord Tang pushed into me.

Mistake. The wolf, who had been calmed by his Keeper, inserted himself between me and Lord Tang.

Lord Tang's hand flew up and was halfway down, but Connor lunged in front of the wolf. A huge red handprint formed as blood welled up across his cheek.

The wolf lunged at Lord Tang, only to be blocked by Aidan and two other Blood Drinkers. The seven others went to surround Connor, but I yanked him behind me, snarling, daring them to attack.

Not sure what they saw, but they took the hint. The beast rode me hard. Wanted to join in on the fun. I longed to show who was the strongest and how little I liked them attacking two of my subjects.

"You can't let them harm him." Connor whispered. "You caused this mess. You knew what would happen when you goaded me."

Hadn't goaded him. Did let his unease go until his Bombardian arrived. Hadn't expected chaos to ascend. Nothing left for me to do but let the shit storm unravel. Gave Lord Tang a preview of what happened when someone messeed with a Bombardian's Keeper.

"Stop this before Robin gets hurt, or Charles gives the order to eliminate him."

"Charles?" I watched as Robin snapped at the man beside Aidan.

"Lord Tang."

"That's his name?" I glanced over my shoulder, cursing the small trickle of blood making its way down Connor's cheek. "Why are you bleeding?"

"Lord Tang . . ." Connor sighed. "He had his claws out when he attacked Robin."

"Damn it." I tugged the handkerchief from my pocket and tossed it at him. "Clean your face. We do not need Robin seeing that."

"Right." Connor pressed the white cloth to his face. "Please stop this."

"Why?"

Stupid question, but I needed to know how far things had gone between Robin and Connor. I knew the mark had been made, but that told me very little. Other than Lord Tang had not picked up on Robin's scent. Not unexpected.

"I don't want anyone hurt."

"Has Robin explained what that mark means?" I watched as Robin's beast pushed in on Aidan and the other two blocking his path to the one who dared strike his Keeper.

"Yes."

"Then why have you not told Lord Tang?"

"I . . . Will you stop this mess if I let Charles know I have made an agreement with your Bombardian?"

Not a Mélange coming my way. Long as I can keep Lord Tang from exploding. Even better was I gained some great knowledge of the Blood Drinkers. They protected their leader. There was a mental connection between Lord Tang and his guards like there were between me and my Combatants. The Blood Drinkers were hesitant about attacking. Was that because they feared Robin's beast, or . . . Were they waiting for him to make a move, which he'd done by snapping and lunging at their leader. Lord Tang remained out of the action for the most part. Made one attack then let the guards take over. Not something a Royal Leader would have done. We charged into the fray and took control of the battle right alongside our Combatants.

"Commander, please."

Ah . . . Robin had explained a lot to his Keeper. Good. "Is he a guard of yours?"

"No."

"Then what?"

Before Connor could answer, Robin's wolf leapt up and latched his teeth around Aidan's leg. Last straw. I had chatted and gained more than expected. Tried to let Robin teach Lord Tang a lesson, but the chaos put my Keeper in danger. Stupid decision. I should have known Aidan, or someone else, would end up hurt. Just like I should have considered Aidan coming to his leader's aid.

"Robin, stand down this minute."

The wolf released his hold and spun towards me, snarling.

Didn't need to be told how the wolf felt. All the wolf saw was people attacking his Keeper and him. He'd been in the right to eliminate them all. Any other time, I would have let him, but . . .

"You have enough to answer for, do you not think." I pointed at my feet. "Stand there until you are calm enough to shift back." I ran my eyes over Aidan and crooked my finger at him.

"Stay where you are, Aidan." Lord Tang crossed his arms. "You have no right to call any of my subjects." He stepped aside, gaining a better sight of Connor. "Come here and let me take care of what your rash actions caused."

Rash actions? All the young man had done was protect his Bombardian. Not rash Brave. Courageous. Stupid, but no way near rash.

"I will stay right here, Sir."

"Connor, that was not a request."

"I," one small step to the right blocked Connor from Lord Tang's view. "It is time that Connor and you spoke. While you do so, Robin and Aidan will need to be present. The rest will have to leave."

"No. The ass wipe just popped in from nowhere. I will not let any of my Blood Drinkers leave until he is off my property." Lord Tang faced Aidan. "Take him to the outer edge and ensure he can not reenter."

Aidan nodded, but frowned as he waved Robin to follow.

Robin looked up at me. One deep breath and a mental sigh did little to settle my beast. "Lord Tang, you brought me here to solve an issue. That is all I was doing. Might have gone about it the wrong way, but it brought the truth to the surface."

"Truth?"

"Yes. From the way Connor was acting and some of his lack of wording told me he knew more than you."

"I truly doubt that."

I stepped aside and waved at Connor. "Tell him."

"There are too many . . ."

Lord Tang must have known Connor well, because he quickly picked up on his unease. Not that it was hard. Connor's voice wavered and water bubbled behind his eyes. Robin's wolf went to his Keeper's side, rubbing his head against his leg. Connor automatically dropped to his knees and rested his head against the wolf's.

"Aidan, stay with us. Rest of you . . . Take your leave."

"You sure, Lord Tang?"

Aidan looked my way and I felt my lips stretch upwards.

"They can leave."

I went back to my seat and Connor walked over to the swing. Robin stayed on his heels and jumped up beside him, placing his head in his Keeper's lap.

Lord Tang hissed but said nothing. He did take his seat.

Aidan came to the banister beside me and hopped up, letting his foot rest against my leg. Wasn't much contact, but enough to let me know he had some interest. Finding out what kind would have to take place after I solved the problem at hand. Not that it was my problem. Then again . . . Might be.

My kind could not afford to alienate a clan of Blood Drinkers before we went public. The human world would have a hard time swallowing the news. Did not need the fact of Blood Drinkers to come to life. Not to mention, Robin made Connor one of my subject when he marked him. Keepers were revered and protected before any other.

Chapter 14

Aidan

Was in the house some time when the commotion broke out. I rushed onto the porch, blocking Robin, or that's who I thought it was. Hard to tell when his face was flickering back and forth between his normal strait-laced appearance and slanted eyes with his nose realigning into what was a . . .

Wolf.

What in the world? Was that why they were called a Bombardian? Sure fit. Pure fact that a person could turn into a wolf sure bombarded my mind. I might have to drink blood, but nothing else shared my body. That would . . . Funky.

None of that mattered. The entire situation had been inevitable. Not because of Lord Tang, but Commander Theodor. It had been more than clear that he baited Connor. Pushed him until his answers revealed that he had broken several of Lord Tang's rules. Wasn't sure why he did so. Was sure the man did not do anything without a reason.

My initial reaction when I jerked the door open was to protect my Inamorato from the guards that was storming the porch. I never made it to him. Things went haywire. Connor threw himself over the wolf, screaming not to harm him. Lord Tang lifted his hands as he extracted his claws. He aimed for the wolf, but he ended up striking Connor. Commander Theodor smoothly jerked Connor behind him as the wolf pressed in on Lord Tang. Wolf gave us plenty of warning before he made contact.

Animal had some sharp, strong teeth. I'd have marks for several days. Shocked me how fast the wolf retreated when Commander Theodor ordered the wolf to stand down. I might not have done so if Lord Tang had harmed Commander Theodor. Would have torn him in half and it would have been my right to do so.

Once the situation was calmer and the other guards had left, I made my way to the banister and hopped onto it, ensuring my leg touched Commander Theodor. Wasn't as much as my body longed for, but it would have to do. Soon as I touched him his shoulders lifted and fell as his eyes drifted over my leg. If I hadn't already known he was attracted to me, I would have then. What bothered me most was how his sexy eyes latched onto my torn jeans. There was little blood, but it ached and would until I retrieved a bag of blood. It was as if . . .

Commander Theodor needed something from me. That became clear when he told Lord Tang everyone had to leave but me and him. What though?

Chapter 15

Theodor

Hands rested on legs. Not at ease pose, which I should have tried to achieve, but my beast was demanding I check on our Keeper. His slight touch helped. Some. Not enough. If he had pulled the touch away, I might have lost control. Thankfully, he kept contact the entire time Lord Tang spoke.

Connor calmly and slowly told Lord Tang that him and Robin had an agreement. Should have had my full attention on that, but I kept glancing at the hottie sitting less than five inches from me. Not what I should have done, because I knew Lord Tang was less than a minute from throwing an enormous fit if Connor had decided to leave the safety of the clan. Then again . . . Robin worked for Lord Tang for some time. Yet . . . Lord Tan had been limiting how much time the two spent together.

"This would be a hell of lot easier," Lord Tang's sharp tone had me sitting up taller. "If the ass wipe would shift back. I can't say what I want to some damn dog."

"Hey!" I was on the edge of the seat. "Watch it."

"Sorry." Lord Tang sighed. "I can't talk to a . . . What do you call yourselves in this form?"

"Wolf." Connor replied.

"Some do." I said.

"Fine." Lord Tang waved his hand at Robin. "Order him to shift."

"It doesn't work that way." Did at times, but when a Keeper was involved . . .

"Why not? He shifted with ease."

"That was out of fear for his Keeper." I crossed my ankles and scooted back in my seat. "Until he is sure his Keeper is safe, he will not be able to calm completely down."

"Then you speak for him."

"Hell no." Not stupid. "Robin is his own man. He speaks for himself. I can tell you this . . ." My words would do nothing to help, but they had to be said. "From what Connor told me, the two have worked out an agreement. My best guest, it included remaining inside your domain." An amazing thing on Robin's part. "I'm assuming your actions were making it hard for Connor to uphold his agreement and they were working on a different one."

Wasn't a common action for most Bombardian and Keeper, but it had happened a couple of time. Neither involved a Keeper having to remain in another species area. Not that I was aware of.

I just hoped I read between the lines right. It sure seemed like what I would have done in Robin's spot. The spot I'm in might be a bit more challenging. One issue at a time. Robin and Connor first. Then Aidan and me.

"That's what I need him to explain." Lord Tang jumped up and paced the length of the porch.

What was there to say? Robin's wolf would not recede until his Keeper was safe. Lord Tang would not calm down until he knew what Robin wanted.

"Commander Theodor," Aidan's rich voice washed over me like butter. "Lord Tang will not settle until he knows what Robin is threatening."

"He is not threating anything." Connor rolled his eyes, making me press my lips together to hold back laughter. "He simply wants us to live our lives. We can not do that if Charles keeps up apart."

"That's Lord Tang to you." Aidan snapped.

"We are not among other Blood Drinkers." Connor patted the top of Robin's head.

"What am I chop liver?"

"You're . . . Aidan." Connor snickered. "You have been Charles friend since before I was born."

Didn't know Aidan well yet, but the barely visible frown told me those words were not the truth.

"Still . . . You are in mixed company. Show him the respect he is due."

"He's fine." Lord Tang flopped into the chair. "I think the best thing we can do for now is let . . ." Lord Tang locked eyes with me. "How long will it take for him to calm down?"

"Depends."

"On what?"

"Who is around. The tension in the air. How close he is to his Keeper. How well his Keeper is at calming him beast's side."

"Beast?"

"Wolf. Beast. Told you we each call our other side as we see them."

"Fine. Fine. If I leave Connor with his guards for the next couple of hours will he be safe?"

"He will be safer with his Bombardian. You have seen we have ways to reach our Keeper within seconds."

"Connor always has guards." Aidan ran the toe of his shoe up the side of my leg, drawing my full attention to his sensual lips.

"Then maybe let them remain outside while Connor and Robin spend some time together. I am not sure when they saw each other last. The longer apart the harder it is for us to control our other side." I stood. "I think I will take the time they need to get settled in to rest a bit" Nothing else I could do. It was up to Robin and Connor. Until Lord Tang and Robin spoke I could not intercede. Not that I would do much of that. The agreement made with a Keeper is between the Keeper and Bombardian. Not anyone else. It was going to be a bit of a battle to get Lord Tang to understand that.

"Fine. Fine. The guards can remain outside." Lord Tang huffed but showed no other disdain. "I'll check back in a couple of hours, Connor."

"Yes, Charles." Connor stood and opened the door. "Come on, Robin. Let's go rest in front of the fireplace."

I walked down the porch steps after Connor shut the door. I'd hoped Aidan would follow, but . . . Made it a couple of feet away before I heard muffled voices, but they were so low I could not pick up anything, even with my enhanced hearing. Might have been a good thing. I needed to reach out to my cousins and see if they'd heard any stories from their Uncles about other species intermingling. Knew they didn't. How would they since they did not know the Blood Drinkers existed. I'd just have to reach out to Uncle Robert and the others.

Chapter 16

Aidan

"What was up with that shit?"

"What you talking about?"

Could have been my action to Commander Theodor or the entire situation with Connor and Robin. Wasn't stupid. Knew Lord Tang had picked up on my reaction to Commander Theodor. Also knew that Commander Theodor's request for me to stay was important. I might have been flirting with my other half, but I also paid close attention to what Connor told Lord Tang about what a Keeper was and how things came to be between him and Robin. What didn't make sense to me was that Connor said that until he turned eighteen Robin would not have known he belonged to him and if he had been over the age of twenty-one Robin would not have known he was his Keeper. I was way past twenty-one. What did that mean for me? Would there be no chance between me and Commander Theodor? Would he even be able to recognize me as his other half? I mean a Keeper was the one who calmed their other side. Allowed them to maintain control. I learned all this, but none of it fit with the spot I found myself in. I knew Commander Theodor belonged to me, but did he know it. Would he know it? Did the age thing not apply to us? We were not of the same species. Damn, what was I to do?

"You are not listening to me."

"I am."

"Then you going to tell me what was taking place between you and Commander Theodor."

"No."

"Not asking. Ordering."

Course Lord Tang went all leader on me. Always did when he was in the dark. Man would not allow such, not every.

"I'm waiting."

An order was an order. Even if I disliked it. Even if I did not want him to know about Commander Theodor's connection to me.

"Do not make me find out on my own."

"You would not dare."

"I will do whatever is necessary to know what is taking place in my domain. You know I will."

He would. I did not need him taking my blood in such a horrific manner. Not to mention no one was to know who my father was. The connection would cause an uproar. It was the one rule I was given when I left my father's clan. No one was to know I grew up under the control of the Hierarchy second. Not because they would come to take me to get their way, but because my dad's job would come to me, if I wanted it. I did not. That's why I left his clan, but I could not officially decline the spot until my father decided to step down.

Lord Tang had a death grip on my neck before I even saw him move. I jerked back, freeing myself from his hold. The shock on his face had me standing up taller.

"You will not do such to me. If you want to know something and it is your business, then I will tell you."

"Everything in my domain is my business. You have never acted so brash before. What has changed since you came in contact with Commander Theodor." His hands flew into the air. "I knew letting that asshole in the area would lead to disaster. I will not stand for it."

I blocked Lord Tang's exit route when he made a move to go for Commander Theodor. "You will not touch my Inamorato."

"You . . . Hell no."

"Yes."

"I forbid it."

"You can not do such."

"I can. So will the Hierarchy."

"No they want. I have done been in contact with them." Not something I wanted him to know, but it was better than him thinking he could manipulate me into giving up my other half.

"When?"

"I knew he belonged to me the moment I saw him."

"When . . . Damn it. I should not have taken anyone with me when I went to him."

"You did. And I'm glad." More than glad. Ecstatic.

"You will not tell him anything about us. Is that clear?"

A ripple of power washed over me. "You did not just . . ."

"I did. You are sworn to me and it is within my right to give you unbreakable orders."

Other words, he was going to make it impossible for me to tell my Inamorato anything about him belonging to me. How was I going to get by this little hiccup?

Chapter 17

Theodor

Halfway down the path footsteps caught my attention. My dick thickened so fast it throbbed. My beast demanded release. Being a Royal Leader was all that kept my hold on it. My two cousins told me how intense their body reacted to their Keeper, but I doubted them. Wrong on my part. Ten times worse.

"Hey! Hey! Commander Theodor, hold up."

I slowed down. Wasn't sure why I didn't stop, but my pace allowed Aidan to catch up.

"Hi."

I slowed more.

"I was . . . Lord Tang . . ."

A hand landed on my arm.

"Thanks for stopping." Aidan's chest rose and fell as he inhaled and exhaled, sending blueberries and vanilla through my entire body. "I'm sorry if I'm bothering you. I . . . I don't have much time." He looked behind him, then back into my eyes.

Why not? Had all the time in the world. Or would once I marked him. That wouldn't be much longer. I hoped. Aidan heard what a Keeper was. The importance of one. That helped. Right?

"Lord Tang . . ."

"What did Lord Tang tell you to inform me of?" I lifted my hand, stopping before I touched him.

"Oh . . . Nothing."

My facial muscles tensed as my eyebrow lifted.

"It was me."

"What was you?"

"The . . . Damn it." Aidan ran his flawless hands across his face. "I wonder . . ." His last words made my beast snarl and howl. Hated seeing those tightly stretched lips and curled up fist pressing hard into his hips.

"Spit it out, won't hurt as bad."

"I can't."

"Why not?"

"Orders."

Ah . . . Lord Tang put restriction on him. Sucked, but understandable. Hoped it didn't hinder me in being able to spend time with him.

"What kind?"

"Can't say."

"What can you say?"

Chapter 18

Aidan

Therein laid the problem. Lord Tang's orders allowed very little. I'd only told him who Commander Theodor was because he ordered me to. Man's *my way* only attitude sucked ass and had my insides shredding. Dire need coursed over me to stand up and demand Lord Tang respect my other half. Such actions would not win over Commander Theodor. Leaders took offense to such actions. Learned that over the years. Wrangling leaders had become a masterpiece of mine. Or wrangling Lord Tang had. Commander Theodor . . . Different. I'd seen that from the first time I saw him. Treating him like I did Lord Tang would not aid me in my quest. Nope. It would drive him away. Might do that anyway since Lord Tang gave me an order that basically sealed my lips with glue. Basically, but . . . There were ways around everything. That had been my purpose of catching up with Commander Theodor. That and the fact he'd been adamant about me being present while Connor explained about Bombardians and Keepers. Knew such information was important, just not how it related to me and him. If it did at all. For all I knew, Commander Theodor wanted the second in command to know what was taking place because he was preparing to eliminate Lord Tang.

Shit. I hoped not. Did not want to have to choose between Lord Tang, my clan, and my other half.

"Can we talk over there?"

Always hated the picnic tables, but right then . . . It was a safe zone. Not inside the cabin Lord Tang placed Commander Theodor in. After Lord Tang orders I wasn't sure if he had bugged the place or not. Would not have put it passed him. Then again . . . Lord Tang had forbidden me from telling Commander Theodor anything about us, including him being my Inamorato.

"Sure."

"Thanks."

With ease I gave Commander Theodor my back, not something I done with anyone, not even Lord Tang. Commander Theodor's vibe that there was something between us put me at ease. Only reason I took the spot that put my back to the woods. It provided me a clear path of sight and I would feel if anyone came up behind us. Least this part of the woods were off bounds to all but guards. Lord Tang despised people going to close to the edge of the domain and this section was only a hop and skip to the end of Lord Tang's area.

Commander Theodor scanned the area and frowned. Did not take a genius to know he disliked the area as well. Why? Woods? Such an open space? Reason did not matter to me. My mind screamed to put him at ease. Make him relax. I could. All I had to do was . . . Tell him, but . . . Lord Tang had no right to order me to keep my mouth shut. I could break the order if I wanted to. I thought. Not knowing how things would work between our two species kept me a bit stand offish.

Commander Theodor took a huge breath and slowly sat on the bench across from me. His shoulders were tense and wide, drawing my attention to his broad chest. How would the skin beneath that blue shirt feel? Silkily? Smooth? Hairy? Would it match his semi-tanned muscle-bound arms, or was it a pale creamy color? What would it feel like to bite down on his nipples? Would it turn him on? Did he even like such touches? Some men hated touch during sex. There would be no sex between us, only making love.

I put my hand under the table and flicked my cock. I'd came to talk. To reassure myself that my Inamorato was at ease. Had everything he needed. Hoped to pick up on what was taking place between us. Couldn't do either if I did not start the conversation.

"How are you doing?"

Chapter 19

Theodor

Easy question. Wanted a deeper one, but . . . I'd let Aidan lead. He knew his limits. Did not want to distress him by asking question he could not answer.

"Can you tell me about yourself?"

A trace scent of man flowed by me, making my cock plump more. Control was harder than hell to maintain, but I had to put my lust out of mind. Smelling it from my Keeper drove my beast wild and my dire need to fuck him higher. I shifted, taking in a deep breath.

"As I'm sure you were told, I am one of five leaders of the Bombardians. Our lives intermingle pretty much every day." I ran my hand up and down my legs, letting the cooling jean material ease my prickling nerves.

"What is a Bombardian?"

"Basically . . . We are human with a beast, or as some call it, wolf."

"How did you get this . . ."

"Beast."

"That's what you call yours?"

I nodded.

"Why?"

My heart raced with need. Need to fuck him. Need to touch him. Need to tell him all, but . . . How much of what I say would get back to Lord Tang. Did not need the Blood Drinkers knowing too much. Then again . . .

Aidan was my Keeper. He had the right to know his Bombardian. Then again . . .

Aidan had no idea he was the one that would calm my beast. The one I craved.

"I feel . . . Tension. Can you not tell me?"

"I want to, but . . ."

"You fear me reporting to Lord Tang."

I nodded even though a sharp pain shot through my entire body, settling in my chest. "I do not know what orders you were given; and you are . . . His second." I hoped that was the right word. "That means you are a protector and you are furiously loyal to him." Fact I despised but understood.

"You are right, but he would never make one of his subjects give details of their . . ." Aidan tilted his head to the left, frowning. "Just trust me."

"Why did you not finish your sentence?"

"Can't."

Damn it. I shoved my hands under my legs and kicked my legs out, hitting Aidan's legs. I went to move them, but Aidan's foot ran up to my knee and back down, stopping on my calf, tucking the toe of his shoe behind it.

"I want to. Really do, but . . ."

"That there is why I . . ."

"I get it. I do." Aidan's foot tugged my leg, causing me to slide further down on the bench. "Just need you to trust me. I would not . . . What if I gave you my solemn oath?"

My cock pressed into my zipper. The light and simple touch had my hips jutting forward. "What is that?"

"It is . . . Does your kind deal with magic?"

An answer to that would not reveal facts. Half-truths stuck to the roof of my mouth and had my beast shoving for control. An evasive answer would work. No omissions. No lies. Respect to my Keeper.

"Sort of."

"Then allow me to use my magic to ensure you that I will not tell anyone what you tell me about you."

"Just me?"

"Your kind in all."

"How does this magic ensure you uphold your word?"

“Once I speak the words there is no way I can break it. My kind upholds their promises no matter the situation. I promise.”

Went into my normal debate pose. My hands holding my chin always put me at ease. Also gave me a perfect line of sight to Aidan’s sparkling red eyes. Had no reason to distrust my Keeper. He smelt of truth. Man was upfront and gave me some facts about his kind, even though he sat up taller and lips were turned down. Wasn’t sure why it seemed to hurt him to do so, but he had. There’d been no restrictions put on me from him. I owed him the same trust. He provided a way for me to do so. I had to show my Keeper that I respected him. The more I gave the further Aidan’s mind would be open to being my Keeper. Right?

“Do so.”

“I, Aidan Jensen, give my word that nothing I learn and am told by Commander Theodor will cross my lips, or be written down, to anyone, not even my Lord.”

A faint breeze ruffled my hair as fresh cut grass filled the air. I’d smelt it many times when David pulled on his affinity. If Aidan broke his word, then . . . Earth would be displeased, and she did not tolerate such actions.

“You used Earth.”

“I am not sure where that skill comes from.”

If there was anything I knew, it was how the affinities reacted to broken promises. Answer enough.

“Ask your questions. I will answer honestly.”

Chapter 20

Aidan

"How did you get your beast?"

Not best place to start, but it was what spilled from me. A tirade of questions and filled my mind and I doubted I'd get time to ask them all.

"We are children born to females with blood Type A and carry an extra chromosome called Type W. It provided our descendant with extra abilities, including a beast side."

"You have more talent than shifting into a beast?"

Commander Theodor smiled at me, making my cock harden more. It was going to burst free if it got any larger. Not sure if it could.

"How did the Type W chromosome come about?"

"Long ago a female with the Type A bared a child after marrying a man that had been experimented on."

Made sense. Not really, but it was as likely as how we came to exist. Least they had a way to prove their creation. Blood Drinkers did not. Our creation came about the same way most humans believe they did. A creator who created them in his image.

"Why did you expose yourself to the humans?"

"We have not. Yet."

"Then why was . . . Those homes created?"

"Destroyer's Hermitages were created by the humans to house the Keepers and Protectors that refused to live a full live with their Bombardians."

"You do not seem like a boogieman. Nor does . . . Nor did Robin."

"We are not. I provoked Robin into to revealing himself. Caused his beast to come out. His actions would not be held against him."

Robin had been ready to tear Lord Tang in half. Not to mention me for getting in his way.

"His actions were my fault."

"How so?"

"I goaded his Keeper."

Lots were said in that answer that wasn't said. Commander Theodor had known what he was doing. He must have been able to read Connor's thoughts. Or something. Connor would not have ratted out Robin. That had been clear in his answers to Lord Tang and what he had kept from Lord Tang. Connor had been doing nothing but standing up for himself, which the young man had never done before. Always shocked me. He was around nothing but Blood Drinkers and a few humans who were loyal to Lord Tang. He had no social skills. Never been allowed out of the domain. Limited action with his own kind. Lord Tang had not done Connor any favors by keeping him secluded. I'd told him that many times, but the jerk wad refused to listen. Just like most of the time.

"You forced Robin's hand." I huffed instead of laughing at the sneakiness. "I take it you would not have done so unless . . ."

"You are right. It is our utmost law to take care of all Keepers and Protectors."

"Right. Because they keep your beast under control." Would I do that since I'm a different race? What if I didn't. Did that mean he would become this half wolf, half human monster mentioned?

"Correct."

Commander Theodor's rich brown eyes bore into me, etching my desire higher and higher. Not only mine from the smell of musk and man. Did that mean I was driving him up the wall as much as he was me? I hoped so. Took all my control to keep my mouth shut about us being paired together in the way of my people, but my gut told me there was something else I needed to know before I opened myself up to Commander Theodor. What though?

"Are these Keepers and Protectors a result of the . . . Experiment?"

"Yes."

"Is there a way you know these people belong to you?"

I ran the toe of my shoe further up his leg, forgoing stopping at his knee, which had me scooting down further on the bench until my shoe reached the edge of his thigh. The closeness put my sole right against his enlarged cock.

"A scent. Their voice. Our reaction to them."

Reaction? Being hard as rock? Was the massive cock I felt the result of . . . A hand came to rest over my foot, slipping under the edge of my pants. Moment his rough hard-working hands made contact with my skin a groan slipped from me.

"Upon meeting them they drive our beast wild. Makes it harder to control them until we have an agreement with them."

"Sounds a lot like . . . Fuck!" Shards ripped through my head, forcing me to squeeze my head until the pressure lessened.

"You okay?" Commander Theodor all but lunged across the table before I could answer him.

"Orders can be . . . Sucks."

Commander Theodor winked at him. "Sort of understand."

"You are a leader, how can you."

"Might be a leader and others might not give me orders, but I had to . . ."

"Had to what?"

The light went out of Commander Theodor's eyes. Pain harder than what Lord Tang's order caused shot through me, making me reach out to him, but my shaking hands hung in the empty space between us. Paleness consumed my Inamorato, sending the urge to tear into whatever distressed him crashed over me. The urge to soothe him and return the peacefulness squashed that urge. I on my feet before I thought things through.

My sudden action had Commander Theodor on his feet. His eyes roamed the area, taking in every corner of the woods behind them.

"What is it?"

I floated over the table, landing right beside him. My arms wrapped around his waist, tugging Commander Theodor against me as my lips closed over Commander Theodor's. There was no gentleness as I demanded he open for me. Soon as his lips gave a small opening my tongue shoved its way into Commander Theodor. Our tongues dueled for control. There was no winner. We both explored each other's mouth, retching up our desire, which had our hips thrusting against the other one's midsection. Theodor up the antics as his hands ran up my spine and down to rest over my ass. Somehow Commander Theodor managed to pull me closer to him. His intense reaction to my action had my natural instinct revved up. Took all the control I had not to slip my lips down the man's neck, piercing his neck and feeding from him. He was my Inamorato, it was the most natural action and sex always boosted a Blood Drinker's need to feed. But there was no way I could let myself do such until he knew who he was to me and I knew just how the Keeper aspect played a role between us.

Was Commander Theodor trying to tell me he had a Keeper and his desire for me would never be acted upon, more than what we were doing at that time? What if he was involved with someone? What did that mean for us? We were fated to be with one another.

My shirt lifted as Commander Theodor yanked it free from my pants. When his hand slipped under the edge of them, I jerked away. There was no way I could do such if the man had a Keeper. No matter how much my body, soul, and mind told me it did not matter. It did.

Before I could break contact with Commander Theodor and ask him, a sharp jolt rocked my body back ten feet, slamming me into a thick, solid tree.

Didn't expect the reaction that took place next.

Commander Theodor screamed as his body contorted so fast that I almost missed his shift. The coat of fur seemed to skin him, making my stomach swirl.

"Shit. Sorry. I'm so sorry. I didn't mean . . ."

Chapter 21

Theodor

I heard my Keeper, but the beast was too busy searching the area for the invader. It stalked around Aidan, snarling and sniffing, finding nothing.

A soft, gentle hand ran across its thick fur, warm soothing air spread across my beast, making it look up. It huffed, sending spittle flying.

Aidan chuckled and knelt. "I'm sorry. I didn't mean to cause this."

I pleaded with the beast to retreat so I could gain an explanation, but the beast refused. Hunt mode rode the beast hard and would until he found who had . . .

"There is no one here. I promise."

My beast snorted and looked towards the tree that its Keeper had been thrown into.

"It was my own fault." Aidan sat down on the grass in front of me, taking my snout in his hand. "I broke an order and was reprimanded."

Intruder. Lord Tang had no idea what he had done. My beast would dig its teeth into the Blood Drinker's guts, ripping them out piece by piece. Would take all my control, and my Keeper, to keep me from doing so. Then again . . .

I might anyway.

"Can you shift back and explain why your beast came forward?"

I shook my head, hating I could not give my Keeper his wish. It would take me some time before the beast would settle down and retreat.

"Is there anything I can do to help calm you?"

Agree to be mine. Come home with me. Meet my cousins. Go through the Pledging Ceremony. All of which I could not tell Aidan. Not just because I was in the body of my beast, but the timing wasn't right. Since I could not say anything, I simply looked towards the path that led to my cabin, tossing my head.

"You want me to walk with you and let you in?"

The beast nodded its head.

"I am truly sorry I cut our time together short."

My beast ran his snout up Aidan's chest and across his cheek, licking him. Aidan wrapped his arms around the beast.

"Your beast is not a beast."

He squeezed me and got to his feet. "Let's go."

We walked down the path and up the stairs of the cabin. Whole time Aidan kept his hands in my fur. He opened the door and smiled down at me.

"I'll come by and see you in the morning. Is that okay?"

My beast nodded and walked inside. The door shut behind him and footsteps faded as the darkness enfolded Aidan. My beast dropped to the floor and took in some deep breaths. It was late and I still needed to visit my cousins. They'd be asleep, but they would have to wake up. A late night meeting was unusual, but required.

Chapter 22

Theodor

"Fuck! David." I froze as a cool serrated blade pressed into my neck. "It's me."

David inhaled. I held my breath until David realized who had popped into his room. Not the wisest mover I'd made. I knew David was on high alert. I would have been to if Aidan carried twins. Would he be able to give me a child?

"What the hell are you thinking?" Bryan ran his hand down David's spine, leaning into David's neck. "Calm down, big guy."

David dropped his arms.

"Good question." David inhaled deeply and lifted his hand when the door flew open. "I'm fine."

I looked over my shoulder as Cain took stance in the doorway. "Oh." He shook his head and walked back into the hallway. Man had always been a great General. He knew when real trouble found his Commander and when one of the cousins pulled a stupid stunt. Purposely, or accidentally.

"What do you need?"

Least Bryan knew how to subdue his Bombardian. Bryan pulled David back to the bed and sat down. Man was the bluntest one I'd ever encountered. Wasn't sure if that was good or not. Sure fit with David.

"I have to call a late night meeting."

"Why?" David leaned his head on Bryan's shoulder, sending my mind right to the problem at hand. "Larry won't like this."

"Why not?"

"He's on the edge of his limit. His blood pressure is going through the roof, causing him to black out."

Shit. Anthony must be having a fit. "You know what's causing it?"

"Tray says it's an affect from the pregnancy. Stress is high, making it worse."

"They came up with a plan for his father?"

Me and David went on discussing the finer points of what Larry believed to be the best approach. They were all set to make the call to the President Wells the next day. Meant I had to keep my phone close incase I was needed for a vote. David feared there would be a shitstorm from the President and not the fatherly kind. I had to agree, but I had my own issues that needed solving before all that happened.

"Will we be able to leave Anthony from this?"

I thought over David's question. David, Caleb, and Franklin were all smart men and I trusted them to come up with the right decision. If Anthony was involved the results could be a tie. Since the issue involved me, my count did not count.

"Don't bother him."

"Something three can take care of, then." David handed Bryan a glass of water from the nightstand, smiling at him, making me long to have my own Keeper in the bed beside me.

"Thanks." Bryan rested his head against David's shoulder as he sipped the water.

Such a simple action warmed my heart and put a dire drive to start the meeting. "How's he doing?"

"Sickness medication is working." David's entire body seemed lighter than when he came back.

"Sorry I bother you, but it is important that I speak with you three."

"Call the others and we can use the office here."

"That's why I dropped into your room." Knew David would not leave his Keeper long enough to visit my house. Until Bryan gave birth, everything would take place at David's.

* * *

Caleb and Franklin hadn't been please with me, but none came in bearing a knife. They'd came in cussing about their nights being interrupted.

"What's up that could not wait until daytime." Caleb shoved his head into the small fridge. "I had a long night of sex planned."

Man always had a man, or woman, in his bed. Franklin was the only cousin that wasn't a sexual prowler. Or . . . If he was, he kept it hidden. Still got a few choice words from him when I called. Nothing more than I expected.

"Sorry. It's been a long day."

"Why?" David sat down at the head of the round conference table.

"You know I'm still the eldest."

"I know, but this is my house, so I sit where I want."

"Get on with it." Franklin laid his head on the table.

"You awake enough?"

"Shit. It's that important?" Franklin shook his head. "Caleb tossed me a bottle of water."

"What's up?" David sat back.

"I found my Keeper."

"Hold up." Caleb sat down. "You went off on an unknown mission, by yourself, without telling us what was going on and you found your Keeper."

A deep breath flowed from me as I replayed each jumbled up word Caleb said, then nodded.

"Then you want permission to don the Red Hooded Guy?" Franklin tapped the table. "I guess we are still doing that."

"We aren't out yet." David sighed. "That's why Anthony was not bothered."

"Wonder where he was." Caleb shook his head. "Better to have three than four."

"Until then we stick with the agreement we have." David leaned forward, glancing up at me. "Right?"

Only option. Even after we come out, the laws would not change right away. Red Hooded Guy was not going anywhere until a full rewrite of an agreement and a full admission of what had taken place all those years ago.

"Correct."

"I still think we need to consider whether we are going to keep the Red Hooded Guy or not. I mean," Caleb waved his hands at them, "we know what is about to go down. Isn't it our duty to lead by example?"

Caleb was right. We led by example, but there was no reversal to the law of the Red Hooded Guy. Yet. Sure, there would be in time, but until then . . . "We stay within the parameters of the law."

"Thought we voted." Caleb shrugged when Franklin huffed. "What? We do. Don't we?"

"We do." David tossed them each a yellow notepad. "Do we stick to the current laws or rewrite it before we are official out to the humans?"

Quick vote. Came up three to one. Caleb didn't say anything, but his smile told me all I needed to know. He'd brought that up to see how I would react. If I was going to want to change things since I found my Keeper.

"That's done." David focused on me. "Now tell me what has been going on."

"What?" I pulled out a chair and sat down, readying myself to admit to my white lie.

"Where have you been? What have you been doing? You left right after my home was invaded."

True. I'd left to take care of the one who brought trouble to David's house.

"Did you find out more about why a Vampire used twisted Bobmardians to attack us?" Franklin squashed his empty bottle and tossed it into the waste basket.

"I did."

"And?"

"They are Blood Drinkers. I don't have much to report on what they are capable of." Did know the group had magical abilities but would not tell what Aidan told me in confidence. "Lord Tang needed help understanding how someone had marked his human ward."

"I'm sure he knew what the Marked Ones were." David huffed. "Or do they not have television or keep up with the human world."

"He did, but he did not understand how the man became marked."

"Why not?" Caleb took a sip of water.

"Apparently, me and Uncle Robert bore an identifiable scent. None of his workers bore that scent."

"We have a scent?" David scowled. "Why did we not know this?"

Theodor shrugged and leaned back in his chair. "Anyway, I solved that problem." Almost caused a battle doing so. My cousins didn't need to know that. There'd be no living that down. Stupid mistake on my part.

"So, we have another Bombardian with a Keeper, or Protector."

"Keeper." Knew Connor and Robin had an agreement, one that was up in the air and that Lord Tang was unhappy about. Not that the Blood Drinker could change it. What was done was done. If he did not agree, I was sure Connor would leave his domain.

"The question is, can Theodor don the Red Hooded Guy." David nodded at each of them.

"Don't think that matters in my case." I'd done let Aidan hear about Keepers and Protectors.

"You have to do what the law requires. We just said that." Franklin went to the fridge, muttering about never getting back to sleep. "We just reinforced the rule that stated all Royal Leaders had to follow the laws every Bombardian went by."

"Depends on the Keeper or Protector." David said before I could remind Franklin of how we'd changed the law when Anthony found Larry.

"Right." Franklin sat down. "What is there to talk about? I think all the unexpected Keepers have been found. I mean who could be more known that the President's son."

Here we went. "Not known." Before any of them could speak I drove forward. "Before we get into things I need to know if David or Caleb was told about interspecies pairing."

"Fuck!" David sprang from the chair. "Your . . . Your Keeper is a Blood Drinker."

Leave it to him to pinpoint the problem quickly.

"Shit. Is that . . ." Caleb shook his head and groaned. "What else has been kept from us?"

"So, you have not heard of this."

"How the hell you think we heard about this?" David snarled. "We didn't even know Blood Drinkers existed."

Just what I thought. Should have gone to Uncle Robert first.

"Pop your ass to your Uncle's and bring him here."

"David," Theodor slumped into his chair. "It's the middle of the night."

"You woke us up."

"Your my cousins."

"He's your Uncle." David crossed his arms.

"You forgetting I have no idea where he lives."

"We have the addresses of all three."

When had we gotten that? Last I heard Uncle Robert and the other two refused to give their location out. They were considered dead by the Bombardians and did not want to admit to the actions of the other two Royal Leaders. The entire Royal Leaders did not need to show there had been discord among their leaders.

"When they realized that we would need the information about how Bryan's pregnancy would go they gave us the information. We promised to keep it between the Royal Leaders."

Not an unreasonable request. One I would have agreed to. Looked as if my fear of the cousins fighting about decisions and having to call him in on every little decision was unwarranted.

"I think . . . David is right." Caleb threw his empty bottle away. "Before we can decide how you need to go about claiming your Keeper we need to know if this has happened before. If it has . . ."

"Give me his number. I'll call him." Hoped the information we got from David's Uncle included phone numbers.

David left the conference room and returned with a sheet of paper. "This has to be tore up soon as you are done with your call."

Not original. I was sure my organized freak cousins had all the information stored somewhere where no one would find it. I'd have to ask later, but then I had other issues to handle.

Chapter 23

Aidan

Tingles raced through each nerve endings, making me spring to my feet.

Get to him. He's gone. He's gone. Where? Why? He left me. How could he? Did he not know. He left me. Gone.

So much more zoomed through me. It had me frozen in place. I knew I needed to get to him. Make him understand what was between us. I knew he felt it. Why else would he have kissed me? His dick was hard as a rock when my shoe rested against it. What made him leave me?

"Move. Damn it." I took two deep calming breaths, or what should have been, and then focused on my feet. "Finally."

The door slammed into the wall as I threw it open and leapt over the porch. Wood cracked, but it did not deter me from flying through the air. Anyone saw me I'd been in trouble. Lord Tang did not allow such use of skills inside his domain. Those, he believed, where meant for battle only. If my other half left me then battle it would be.

I did not bother to knock, I simply opened it with a wave of my hands and flew inside. I sniffed, hoping my body's reaction was wrong.

"Commander Theodor."

Calling his name had been useless and stupid. There was no heartbeat inside the house. He did not come running when the door was open; and he would have known. Man was a leader. His sense would be on high alert in a new location and surrounded by the unknown.

"Why did you leave?"

My teeth clanked as fire seethed under my skin. I paced the living room, questioning every move I'd made. Where had I gone wrong? Listening to my leader. Wanting to find out if an interspecies pairing had ever been heard of? Discovering if I would be able to be with him without disrupting . . . That had to be it. What had I been thinking? Course my entire life would be disrupted. Commander Theodor was a leader of his people. He could not come to live inside the domain and under another strong leader. Wasn't something I could have asked him to do. He would have been unhappy doing such. I knew it. Why had I not thought of it before?

I flopped onto the couch and let my head fall into my hands. Tears bubbled behind my eyelids, but I refused to let them fall. I wasn't a man that cried. I was a man of action. I was a man who made plans. That's what I needed. A plan. What though? I did not know where he lived among the humans. I'd only been outside the domain twice since I came to Lord Tang's area. Before that I'd lived among humans, but everything was different from then. Not only technology, but daily movements and the typical way of life.

"What am I to do?"

Chapter 24

Theodor

The phone call was short and full of cussing. Or the first attempt had been. When I called right back, Uncle Robert demanded to know what was so important. Not that I hadn't expected such a reaction. After all, it was one o'clock in the morning. Uncle Robert demanded to know why I tried to pull such a joke. Took three attempts to explain it was no joke. Line went dead and Cain came in with Uncle Robert right behind him.

"Commander David, he showed up in your hallway."

Uncle Robert walked around him, shrugging before he nodded at David.

Cain didn't respond, just left and shut the door. Man sure made a top notch General and knew his job. Them being best friends before David came into his seat of power helped as well. They knew each other and how they thought and worked.

"Guys," Uncle Robert locked eyes with me and ordered me to explain again.

I quickly recapped Lord Tang's actions, Connor and Robin's pairing and how I met Aidan. Made sure to include how there was something my Keeper tried to tell me but had been ordered to keep his mouth shut.

"Lord Tang was tight lipped when I met him." Uncle Robert sat down beside me. "You sure your Keeper has been ordered?"

I nodded.

"How come?"

"He told me."

"How do you know he is not lying?"

"He was thrown into a tree while we were kissing."

"Reprimanded." Uncle Robert stared up at the ceiling. "Think I need to pay a visit to Lord Tang."

"Don't think that would be allowed." I recalled all the rules Lord Tang put on me. "I barely got permission to pop out to speak to you guys. The Blood Drinker is guarded. "So much I fear his reaction when I mark Aidan.

"Then how are you going to get away with marking him." Franklin had taken to pacing the conference room while I was on the phone with Uncle Robert.

"Can you even mark him?" Robert folded his hands in his lap. "He is another species. We have only marked humans."

Damn. Hadn't considered the marking not taking. What would I do if it did not work? Would Aidan believe me if I outright told him? He'd want proof. I would have. Lord Tang would accuse me of lying to gain control of his second in command.

"The wording would have to be changed."

"How so, David?" I pushed back from the table and made my way to the fridge, opening it and frowning. "Do you not have any beer here?"

"Caleb drunk the last one last night." David said. "The wording doesn't include any specific species, but if you add something about his race then it would pinpoint who you are marking."

"Still . . . It might not work." Uncle Robert sat up taller. "Our skills come from our affinity."

"Yes, but . . ." David leaned forward, "we pull from our ancestors and affinity. I believe that even though we were created by an experiment, an of herb, of some kind, provided by Earth was used. The humans believe they were created from dust of the ground, so why would Blood Drinker not have such belief."

Was David right? I never considered such. Just assumed an experiment created us. Never asked what was used.

"That is slim." Caleb said.

"It is." Uncle Robert added.

"It might be but was I not right all the years I said I would find a Keeper."

He had been. Man never gave up on his dream. He was the first of the Royal Leaders to find a Keeper. Or that we have known of. Could I risk not trying David's theory was thin . . . Extremely thin.

"It's worth a shot." Franklin returned to his seat. "I mean what's the worst that could happen. It fells to work."

Weren't many options. Rewording the marking spell. Tell Aidan and hope he believed me. Hope Lord Tang accepted my word.

"What if he cast the spell and it backfires on his Keeper?" Caleb threw his empty bottle away. "It's a risk either way. What is the least risky way?"

"Maybe he needs to create a brand-new spell that pulls directly from his affinity only." Franklin added.

"What if all five of you cast the spell, wording it so each one of you pull from your affinity. "Uncle Robert nodded. "I think that might be best. Less risky."

"How so?" I wasn't sure how using all five affinities would aid more than pulling directly from Fire."

"We don't have all five here." David sprang to his feet when the door opened and Cain stuck his head inside. "Commander Theodor, Bryan needs you."

David rushed from the room, not bothering to inquire as to why. I looked around the room, stopping on Caleb's face.

"Our meeting are being interrupted when Bryan has a bad throwing up spell."

"Does David not feel his distress?"

"Bryan's learned how to block him. He hates interrupting him when he's working."

Selfless man. Kind of dangerous if he did so when danger came his way. David would not forgive himself if Bryan was harmed in any manner. Even because of his own self.

"That's why one Combatant is stationed outside the room Bryan is in."

David used his guards to spy on his Keeper. Wise.

"What do you mean you don't have all affinities here?" Uncle Robert brought them back to the matter at hand. "What?" he snapped when I glared his way. "David will come back when his Keeper is tended to."

"It's fine, Theodor." Caleb tapped the tabletop. "We can't stop every time he has to run. He's agreed for us to keep going and fill him in when he gets back."

"You sure?" I disliked leaving him behind.

"I am." Caleb looked at Uncle Robert. "Anthony is tied up with his pregnant Keeper."

"Right. Right. Tray told me he had some blood pressure issues. The medication not working."

"There's so much stress from his ordeal with his father that it's not working."

I knew it was bad, but there was no way they could protect Larry from all the stress his dad threw his way. The President was going to be a handful to handle and there was no way they could reveal themselves to the public without Larry's aid. But . . . There was no way we could put his child at risk. Nope. We'd have to forgo coming out to the humans. Then again . . . I doubted Larry would agree to that. The man was as stubborn as Bryan.

"Call him in. He has a responsibility."

"We agreed to handle things without him until Larry was better. He's got enough on his plate when dealing with his father-in-law and Larry's determined that the humans will discover what his father has hidden."

I would have done the same. At the time there should not have been any major issues that came about. Then again . . . I had not counted on my Keeper belonging to another species. That didn't bother me. It honored me that my Keeper was a strong, solid man, even if he was a Blood Drinker.

"Okay. Have David tap into Water. He can."

True. David pulled on all five elements when we lost two Royal Leaders. It all but saved one but putting insides back in place was more than any affinity could accomplish.

"I can do that." David retook his seat.

"Bryan okay?" I glanced at David, who nodded. "You sure you can do that while Bryan is so dependent on you. Last time you did so you were weak for several days." Any Bombardian using their affinity is weakened to some extent. Pulling on more than one would double the effects.

"I'll only need Water. Last time I tapped into all five."

"If you are sure then . . ."

"We have to vote." Franklin sat back. "First we need to add such an act to the rules."'

"Right." I would not ask my cousins to go against our laws. Not even for my Keeper. "David the balls in your court."

"Okay." David slid the yellow notepads and pens towards Caleb and Franklin.

"You guys need me anymore?" Uncle Robert stood.

"Rest is up to us. "David tore a sheet off the note pad.

Uncle Robert didn't say anything else, he simply zapped himself home.

"Man of few words." Franklin snorted. "David put the rule into question."

I picked at my fingernails while David worked over the wording. Then it would be time to decide when was best to cast it. I lost track of time and when David's voice drew me away from my runaway thoughts of how everything could backfire I all but jumped.

"Question at hand . . . Is it acceptable to pull on all five elements and reword the marking spell in order to mark a new species? Two yes carry the vote."

David managed to work it so that all the questions was included in one vote. Not sure I could have done as well. I would have broken it down into more than one vote. One would have been, could one mark another species. Two would have been, could a Royal Leader be paired with another species. Three would have been, could the wording of the marking spell be changed. Then I would have dropped the biggest one, could all five affinities be used to mark another species. David covered all those in one question. Man was good. My faith in David had not been misplaced. Thank God.

I held my breath as I watched the three of them write their answer down and fold the sheets of paper. Didn't even take one when David began unfolding each sheet. Felt like hours passed.

"You can breathe." David smiled. "Let us know when you are ready, and we will help you attempt marking your Keeper." He stood and held his hand out. "Congrats cousin."

I shook his hand, accepting words of encouragement from the others.

Chapter 25

Theodor

"This is becoming a habit." Caleb snorted and held out the small bowl of herbs that David kept on his table.

"I don't think so." David jerked the bowl and stick from me, shaking his head." This is the one I used to mark Bryan."

Lord. Rolling my eyes would have been the right response, but I understood why the piece held such value. I would cover the one I used to mark Aidan in gold and place it in the center of my mantel over the fireplace with a label underneath it. David on the other hand never seemed like sentimental kind. Guess I was wrong about that as well. Been that way on a couple of issues lately. Time I started to give my cousins the credit they were due.

"Has to be one that I can keep."

"Knew that." David held out an older looking herb crushing bowl and stick. Wouldn't have been my first choice, but . . . Couldn't be picky. "We thought it would be stronger if we all lined up in the order of our age."

Whatever they said. The non-existing spell would have to be documented and cemented in our laws. For once . . . I was taking part in it instead of leading it. David had the lead since he was the second eldest. Wrong. David and Caleb shared that responsibility, but Caleb seemed to be letting David take the helm. Didn't bother me. David was a smart man.

"Have you written it down?" I tossed in the mushrooms and began twisting the handle until it was grounded powder.

"Course he has." Caleb held out a sheet of paper. "I was adjusting my part." He tapped the table in front of us. "Don't make it into powder."

I pulled the pedestal up. "Why not?"

"David thinks it will be best if you char them a bit."

"How come?" I felt my forehead crinkle as I looked at David.

He shrugged. "I guess . . . I was thinking it would be best if we each attached a bit of our affinity to the mixture."

"He also thought," Franklin grinned, "that it best if you did not don the Red Hooded Guy costume."

"What?"

"Well . . ." David tapped his fingers. "Your Keeper is not human. We will be addressing the spell to accommodate his race and we are in no agreement with the Blood Drinkers and keeping our identity hidden."

Made sense. Aidan, and all of Lord Tang's clan knew about Bombardians. Why keep up the front when there was no need.

"Does this mean we will be keeping others from seeing me explain what he is to us?"

"I," David tilted his head, "Overall. Won't hurt for other Bombardians to hear. Or other Keepers or Protectors. But . . ."

Flopping in the chair might have been a bit childish, but it took time to take in what my cousins said.

"You think we still need to hold back on how much Blood Drinkers know?"

David nodded. "You said no other Blood Drinker was around when Connor explained who marked him. You also led me to believe that he did not go into details about how Robin came to him, and . . . Connor only mentioned the two of them were . . . Linked to one another for life. That he would either be with Robin or leave. Right?"

Connor had refrained from going that far, but it'd been implied. Wise move to keep Lord Tang in the dark about that fact. Lord Tang discovering he'd hired a Bombardian and not known it put the Blood Drinker at his explosion point. Not to mention I was sure Lord Tang despised that the entire marking took place under his nose. Connor also kept how long he'd been marked to himself. If the two had an agreement, then I was sure Robin marked Connor at least a week or two before Lord Tang saw it. If not longer. The winter months had lasted longer than normal, giving Connor a reason to wear long sleeves late in the year. Showed how much Connor knew Lord Tang.

"Okay." I picked up the bowl and stared into the crushed herbs. "You think we need any different herbs in the mixture?"

"No." David stood up taller. "All we need to do is each speak our part to pull on our affinity and ask for the affinity to answer by effecting the mixture."

"You," I stood, "will be doing Anthony's part?"

"Yes. It will be the last part of the spell."

"Not me?"

"No." David motioned for me to take the spot beside Caleb. "It is best you start the spell and let me end it."

"You aren't sure if you can tap into the affinity?"

"I am." David took one step forward and locked eyes with me. "Cousin, we will ensure that you mark and get accepted by your Keeper. I promise you."

Was it a promise David could ensure? Ultimate choice was up to Aidan, not David.

"Okay. Let's begin."

"First," Caleb handed me the paper. "Read over that and see if you agree with the order and wording."

Some of the wording seemed redundant, but that was typical when pulling on affinities. What I didn't understand was why David inserted the *still agreement* aspect. There had never been a reversal of pairing. Why did he think there might be? Yet . . . No Bombardian, far as we knew, had ever been combined with a Blood Drinker. What if the affinities decided that Aidan and I no longer belong together? That would . . . Rip me apart. I'd started . . . No. If the affinity had done so I would not have felt the connection. Unease and distress flowed through me and it was not mine. It took all my strength not to leave and rush to him. That would not be taking place unless . . . Our connection had already begun to form. But . . .

"David, before you marked Bryan did you feel his unease?"

"You know I did."

Right. He'd known the moment Bryan's parent had not accepted his return. Anthony had known when Larry was overwhelmed before he knew about Bombaridans.

"You already have a connection to him." Franklin rubbed his head. "David, I told you."

"What!" Hadn't meant to shout and I got a furious growl from David.

"Keep it down. Bryan is asleep." David huffed. "Franklin suggest that the marking might not be required at all."

Huh? Never thought of that, but . . . "Why?"

"I . . . There was something you said when you were here. We all skimmed over it, even you. It made me wonder if maybe there was . . . Some kind of . . . Someone like our Keepers for the Blood Drinkers."

I'd skimmed over it then, but I had a similar thought while me and Aidan talked earlier. I'd not gotten time to ask Aidan before Lord Tang threw him into a tree.

"He might be right." David nodded and sighed. "I think it would be . . . Not wise to take the chance. Marking your Keeper is the best approach to take. Best way to ensure you and your Keeper have a chance."

"I agree."

Might have been different if Lord Tang had not shown his dislike of me knowing details about the Blood Drinkers. Not to mention Aidan had been ordered not to tell me facts that pertained to us. If Lord Tang went that far . . . What was to keep the protective leader from going as far as to forbid Aidan from becoming involved in any manner with me. I would not chance that. If Aidan bore my mark, then . . . Made it harder for Lord Tang to interfere. I hoped.

"Okay." David motioned for Franklin to move back into place and I followed suit. "Theodor, start us off and then we go down the line, ending with Spirit."

"Got it."

I squared my shoulder and took a deep breath, silently praying that things went in my favor. With practiced ease fire bubbled to life under my skin.

"Fire, I ask your assistance in marking Aidan, My Blood Drinker Keeper. Give me proof of your acceptance and agreement of the interracial combining by charring the herbs required to shake the ground and blur others."

The flame shot up to my eyebrows and spun in a circle twice before the ground groaned and shapes began to form in front of me. I knew it was the living room inside the cabin Lord Tang assigned to me. The picture began to clear, giving me a scrambled view of Aidan. Unexpected. What was he doing there?

Aidan jumped to his feet. Soon as he saw me, his entire focus was on me. What got me was the redness on his cheeks.

I passed the paper to Caleb, taking the shift of Earth as proof that Fire approved our coupling.

Caleb spun his finger in the air an spoke his part. "Wind, I ask for assistance in bringing down the strength of my eldest ancestor, Edward Lincoln, the first Bombardians born to a Protector. Royal Leader Theodor's Blood Drinker Keeper, Aidan, has been revealed and needs to be awoken to who he is. A Royal Keeper. If you still agree in their interracial combining, then ruffle the herbs inside Royal Leader's Theodor's mortar.

A small white spiral of chard herbs formed inside the bowl I held. Aidan's mouth hung open as if he was asking a question, but no sound came through. I assumed it would come after David recited his part, earning acceptance of Earth like Wind and Fire had.

David took the sheet of paper and lifted a twig from the bowl. "Earth, I ask for assistance in marking Royal Leader's Theodor's Royal Keeper, Aidan. If you still agree with this combining, then refurbish the herbs within the mortar."

Before David finished his request, the mushrooms had reformed into tiny pieces and small bits of crushed up herbs brightened into a new green herbs. What I liked most was how Aidan grabbed his forearm and stared. It pleased me that David waste no time in adding in Anthony's part.

"Water, I ask for assistance in easing Royal Keeper Aidan from as much pain as the unexpected news creates. If you still agree with their coupling pleas give us a sign."

I gasped when water shot up all over my shirt. I glanced at David, who shrugged and muttered an apology. If David had more practice on tapping into his cousin's affinity, I might have been pissed about getting soaked. There were limited number of times he had to do so, and I wanted to keep it that way.

I wiped my shirt as Franklin said his part, ending the spell.

"Spirit, I ask for a show of approval of this new spell and unusual coupling. If you agree then give us a symbol of our Direct Descendant Edward Lincoln's acceptance."

The photo David kept of Edward Lincoln on the table floated towards us and came to rest on the tabletop as I heard the most wonderful words.

"I knew it."

Chapter 26

Aidan

What in the world? What was going on? Mist cocooned around me, sealing me away. Magic rippled over my skin, welcoming me like a mother did a newborn child. A feeling I'd only felt once before. My father told me it was rarely experienced, because most people aren't that in-tune with their true self. He promised it was a gift and I would know how to use it when it awoke. It was like a rocket of knowledge zoomed through me and my body took on motion of its own.

My hand covered my arm, sealing in the burning racing over my forearm. I did not need to look down to see the mark forming on me. It was the same one that graced Connor's. It signaled that I'd been right. Commander Theodor had known I was his. He might not have known about Blood Drinkers and Inamorato, but he felt the connection. From what Connor had said Robin had known the moment he saw him and had marked him within an hour of his eighteenth birthday. Connor had been ticked that Robin left his birthday party before it ended, but that had become nothing soon as the mark appeared on Connor's arm. So . . .

Why had Commander Theodor waited so long? He could ask me the same thing. I had not told him the moment I met him. Would that bite me in the ass? Could it have been that there had never been a pairing such as ours? I knew that fact. Had he had to research it, like I did? Or had he had to reach out to his fellow leaders. From what little I overheard I knew that there were five Royal Leaders and they worked as a majority rules society. It had been clear that Commander Theodor worked as one with his fellow rulers. That could have been why he'd not marked me right off the bat. Could not get pissed over that.

Could not get pissed over anything. He had marked me as his. I would stand at his side. I wasn't sure how that would work out, but . . .

Four imagines took shape, but the one that had my attention was the tall drink of water that had me hard all day. That had ticked me off by leaving the domain without telling me. None of that mattered. I'd been right.

"I knew it."

Stupid comment to make, but it's was all that I could get to come out.

Chapter 27

Theodor

Couple of snorts and a chuckle flowed through the room. Had to give it to them for keeping their . . .

"He's smarter than you, Theodor."

There it was. A jab at my expense. Comedian Caleb never knew how to keep his mouth shut.

"Shut it." David patted my shoulder as he walked by. "We will leave you two to talk."

"How come you three can see him.

Not sure if I moved to Aidan's side, or if he moved to mine, but his warm hand soothed the ire at my cousins seeing my man. It should have just been me seeing him. A marking was a private experience. Had to be the change in the spell that caused the unexpected hiccup. Small one.

I spread my fingers across his forearm, taking in the charred skin, warming Aidan's arm. With ease I traced the sideward W, pausing over the lavender cursive like writing.

"Fire, I ask that you ease my Keeper's forearm."

If there had been pain, Aidan showed no sign of it. Right the opposite. A huge smile graced his sexy face. He bit at his bottom lip and had wide eyes. Clearly, his outburst hadn't been expected. Nice though. None of that took the dire need to ease my man. All I wanted for him was pure happiness.

"Thanks." Aidan wrapped his fingers around mine. "What do you mean how come they can see me?"

Right.

"Where they not supposed to?"

"Not sure." Those blood red pupils had my dick pumping up like a balloon being filled with helium.

"Your kind marks people all the time. Don't you?"

"Me and you . . . We are not the same as other Bombardians and Marked Ones." With eyes locked onto his, I brought up his forearm and ran my tongue over the charred skin. The darkness of it would fade, but until then . . . "I love seeing this mark on you." Would love it more when my name was added to the mark. "It worked." My breath rushed from me, but I didn't recall holding it. My chest hadn't burned like it and I'd been talking, so I hadn't been. But the air rushed from me so fast and hard that I ruffled Aidan's bangs as I leaned over and claimed his lips.

Not my wisest decision, but my cock and beast had been dead set on tying Aidan to me for the rest of our lives.

"Wow!" Aidan's red eyes shined with lust as he swayed from side to side. His Adam-apple bobbed as he took in two deep breaths, shaking his head. "What worked? How come we are different?"

I looped my arm around his waist and walked us over to the sofa. "Rest while I tell you what the Mark means."

"I know. It is the same as Connor's."

Was. Wasn't. Made it hard to explain. Mine and his relationship would be extremely different. Robin and Connor's would . . . Might not be. The gist of being a Keeper would be the same, but if Aidan refused me then . . . Nope. Don't go there. Negative thoughts had no life in my mind. The connection had begun forming. Wouldn't have unless Aidan wanted me in his life. Or that's how it had been for David and Bryan. Yet . . . Bryan had been human.

"Hey," Aidan ran a finger down my cheek. "Ours is different than theirs. Isn't it?"

"I . . . Am . . ."

I hated not being sure. There was no history to tell me what would come. Wasn't even sure if I would have to be with my Keeper to keep my beast calm. The reverse might occur as well. What if I had to be around him more than most Bombardians? What if Aidan decided to forget the Destroyer Hermitage's? Would I still go Mélange? Too many unknowns. My entire body shook. What if I had made a mistake marking my Blood Drinker Keeper? Didn't feel like one, but . . .

"Hey. Hey. Theodor, babe, it's all right. Take a breath. That's it. Another."

Six deep breaths later and my mind slowed, letting the tension clinging to my muscles loosen. It was then I realized Aidan ran his hand up and down my spine, whispering that everything would work out for us. That the connection was a two-way streak. That he would make sure he kept his Inamorato.

"What is that?" I arched my back into Aidan's touch.

"A Blood Drinker's male lover." Aidan's hand drifted over my shoulder, under the back part of my collar, tracing my bare skin. "It is like your Keeper or Protector."

So . . . There was an other half for the Blood Drinkers. Was their connection as in-depth as a Keeper and Bombardian? Did that mean . . . Could Aidan be away from me for a long period of time? If so . . . Would he go insane? Or something worse?

"An Inamorato is a special gift for a Blood Drinker. Only one out of twenty find theirs."

"How many Blood Drinkers are there in the world?"

"About five thousand or so." Aidan rubbed the palm of his hand over my chest, pulling a deep groan from me. "That's why I told Lord Tang. He was not happy, but . . . He has no right to come between an Inamorato and Blood Drinker."

He done had. His order to keep me in the dark about what I was to him done that. Lord Tang had gone as far to harm Aidan when we got too close.

"I know I let him go a bit further than I should have." Aidan rested his head on my shoulder. "I should not have. Should have stood up to him from the start. Made sure you knew what you were to me. If I had then . . ." His hand slid down my chest and came to rest over my abs for a heartbeat before it moved further down. "You might have marked me long before now and I could have made it known to the rest of the Blood Drinkers and the world that we belonged to one another. You are mine. I am yours."

My beast roared it pleasure and pushed for me to take him right then and there, but I knew that wasn't the right course to take. As much as I wanted to.

I gripped Aidan's wrist, stopping him from unbuckling my belt. Not that I didn't want us to go further, but I had to make sure my Keeper understood the full impact of what a Keeper meant."

"Do you . . . Did I misread . . ."

"No." I twisted so I sat sideways, gaining a direct line of sight of soft blue eyes. Where had the red gone? Later. Important things first. "I need you to understand what being a Keeper entails and how it will change your life." And then I need to know how being his Inamorato would affect mine.

"Oh." Aidan sat back, nodding. "Go on. It won't change my mind."

I hoped not.

Chapter 28

Aidan

"A Keeper is the one that calms a Bombardian's beast. Once the two meet they must remain in contact . . ."

Aidan waited while Theodor organized his explanation. It was kind of sexy to hear him explain things to me, when I could feel his fear. I might have asked him what scared him, but I didn't have to. I knew. How could it not. We were in new territory. I was sure what was normal for most Bombardian pairings would not apply to us. How could it. I was not human. Still, I could feel Theodor's need to explain what should take place. Not like it would not aid me. Even if all I wanted to do was get on my knees and shove my ass against him.

"A Keeper or Protector is the one person who calms a Bombardian's beast. Not just anyone can be one though. Each Bombardians is paired with each other for life. If the Keeper or Protector refuses to remain in their Bombardian's life it leaves him in a half state. A state of . . . The Bombardian will lose control of his beast and become stuck in a half-shifted state."

Unease was written across Theodor's masculine, sexy face. I could all but see inside his mind. He would not like how open he was, but I had a feeling this was just another unexpected aspect of our pairing. I knew an Inamorato could be that open to their other half and from what Connor told Lord Tang him and Robin were deeply connected, but he did not mention being able to see and feel Robin's emotions.

"This is . . . You mean . . . I could . . ." I ran my hand over his face, "this is more in-depth than . . . Why did Connor not tell Lord Tang this?"

"His reason is his own." Theodor sat up taller and squared his shoulders. "I hope you will keep that and the rest of what you learn to yourself." He gave me no time to agree or disagree. Kind of cute. "This is why more than ninety five percent of Bombaridans and Keepers or Protectors end up in a love relationship."

Made sense. Such a deep connection would lead to an intense relationship that would expand further than friendship. It would become a hardcore partnership that required them to be in-touched with every aspect of each other's lives. Nothing I did not expect.

"So . . . It's like an Inamorato." I sat back and took a huge breath, because my mind knew better. . . "Except . . . It's not."

"We give our Keeper and Protectors three choices, basically." Not something an Inamorato was given. They were expected to go to one another. It was natural as breathing. "You can accept me as your Bombardian and chose to live with me at your side for the rest of our lives. If you do this . . . We can work out a plan that will accommodate my way of life with yours." That would be hard as hell, but Theodor seemed sure we could do such. Not like I was giving up my other half. Not on my life, but Theodor needed to say his peace. "If you do not wish then . . ." Didn't need him to tell me that that options could not apply to me. I wasn't stupid. I was second in command and if Lord Tang found his Inamorato he would not stash them away in some housing system. Everyone would take it as an opening to take out a powerful leader by eliminating his other half. Not to mention, there was no way I could live there and keep my race hidden. That was an aspect that even the higher ups would not allow. Not to mention there had been a promise made to Lord Tang. I knew all this, but Theodor was struggling with something and I could not aid him with until he was ready to let me. Didn't mean I couldn't push a bit.

"What is it?" I lifted his hand and kissed his knuckles, letting my tongue run across them.

"I just . . . I need to . . ." Ah . . . Theodor was in a tight spot and did not like his options. He gave a short nod and locked eyes with me. "You are not a typical Keeper." He squeezed my fingers. "Your choices will be different."

"I assume as much." I let my hand began to kneed Theodor's palm. "What are mine?"

"You can either agree to be my full time Keeper, which means you and I will sit down and work out a way for my life to fit yours."

"And vice versa."

I hoped it was doable. I knew both of us would do our best, but one fact would never change. We both would need to know that each other was safe, at all times, and from all threats.

"If we can't come to an agreement then what will my choices be?" I ran my hand up to his elbow and gripped it while he feathered his thumb back and forth against the inner side of my arm.

"You can refuse me completely and go back to living your life among your clan."

"Is that what the humans would have done?"

He shook his head. "They would have the choice to have their memories wiped of everything and everyone they knew and start a new life far from their family and Bombaridan."

"Where would me refusing you leave you?"

I knew the answer, but . . . I felt Theodor's desire for me to have all the facts. I believed that he was so full of fear of being rejected and the unknown of what would take place between us that he could not feel I had made my decision before he began to explain.

Might have been wrong, because my question had Theodor holding his breath as his entire body shook. His nose shifted from a human nose and a snout. I had upset him, and he was losing control of his beast. That hadn't been my goal. I could not let him shift. We had to come to an agreement so that Theodor could relax and so could I.

"Theodor, babe, relax." I ran my hand up and down the inner side of his arm. "Breath. In. Out." I kept him focused on his breathing until we were synced. "There you go, babe. Nice and easy for me." I leaned forward and place a light kiss on his forehead. "I would never condemn you to a half-life. There is no way I could do that to my Inamorato."

"You sure about that?" He doubted me. Why? I felt the unease coursing through him, but it made no sense. I wasn't seeing what caused him to fear me leaving him in some kind of unstable state. "Do you know what it truly means?"

"I know what it means."

"You think you can give up your life inside your clan and come join me in ruling the Bombardians?"

Ah . . . That was what he feared. Could see why he would. It was a lot for me to give up. But I knew that one of us would have to give such, and there was no way I could force him to put his kind in such an uproar. I never wanted to be a leader. I could have been several times over, and rejected it every time, so leaving the clan would be hard, but more than doable. Take some adjusting, but I was capable of doing so. It was born and bred in me. Just like Bombardians caring for and protecting their Keepers or Protectors. It was basic and simple. Way of life.

"I do."

"Why?"

"It is our way of life. It is what my Inamorato needs of me."

"It is my job to ensure you are happy at all times. Is that doable with you being apart from your clan?"

"I do not need my clan to have a full life." I scooted onto his lap, looping my arms around his neck. "Most of my kind do not live in clans anymore."

"Then why . . ."

"Lord Tang is one of the oldest Blood Drinkers alive and he prefers things the old ways. For most part."

"You do not?"

"Does not matter to me, long as I have you at my side."

"You sure?"

"Yes." I kissed his cheek. "What do I have to do to accept your as my Bombardians?"

"First, fill me in on what an Inamorato is."

I rushed through how an Inamorato was the other half of our souls. How it was our job to care for, protect, provide, ensure everything they desired. Or to the best of our ability. Pretty much what a Keeper or Protector was, except an Inamorato did not calm us. It was a Blood Drinker's responsibility to keep himself in-line. No one else could make such a decision for him or her. Then there was the fact that the Blood Drinker was there protector twenty-four seven, which I would not have to do. We would protect each other. We would have to agree that each of us could aid one another if trouble arose. Not an unreasonable request for me to make. One I was sure Theodor would give me. Theodor would understand that it was my nature to protect and guard my other half, just like it was his nature to do so.

"I know it won't be easy on you." I massaged the back of his neck. "I'm sure there will be challenges that arise, but we can face them together and head on. Can't we?"

"Sure we can."

"Is there anything else you need to know about?" I ran the tip of my nose over the outer edge of his ear. "If not . . ." My teeth caught the tip of his nose as I pulled back. "There is something I would love to taste."

"Shit." Theodor's groaned and tugged me closer to him. "There is our agreement. It must be made before we seal our relationship."

"How do we seal us together?" I pressed my jean clad cock into his stomach, getting him to thrust up. "Like that, is it?"

"It is, my love." Theodor grasped my ass and pressed me closer to him. "I can't wait to get between these."

"Can't wait for you to either." I nipped his neck and ran my tongue over it. "You going to let me mark you as mine?" Everything inside me screamed for me to place my tattooed fangs on his neck. It would be the one thing that I hoped Theodor could agree to, and quickly because it was taking all my control to keep from feasting on him. I was unsure if I could avoid drinking from him when he made love to me. That was what scared me. It was the one fact I left out, but I knew Lord Tang had told Theodor's uncle that they only fed from blood banks or their other half. I prayed that Theodor's uncle told him that. If not . . . I'd face that when it came up. If it did.

"What's that mean?"

"My fang marks for all Blood Drinkers to see."

"You bite me?"

"Yes."

"You drink from me?"

"Yes."

"Need to do so, daily?"

"Want to, but you can refuse, and I would only do it the one time to mark you."

Theodor tilted his head to the side and smiled at me. "Take what you need and want whenever you want to."

Chapter 29

Theodor

Fangs scraped across my neck, pulling a long, deep groan from me. Those pointed teeth stopped at the base of my neck. A tongue spiraled around and around, pausing a second before a sharp sting consumed my mind. Not pain laced, but one that drove my already throbbing dick into another realm of life. My hard-on doubled, spewing my load right in my pants before Aidan swallowed the first taste of me. I'd be embarrassed over it at some point, but right then . . . My mind opened and Aidan's soft caring tone filled my head.

You are mine for the rest of our lives. What you need is what I will give. You will be the upmost concern in my world. No one will come before you. I am yours. At your beck and call for every breath you take and when your time is no more, mine will cease as well.

Damn. Never considered such an oath would come with Aidan marking me. And what was up with hearing him so clearly inside my head. I mean I knew I'd feel him when we completed the Keeper ritual, but . . .

"Now . . ." Aidan shoved me back until I was laid out under him. "For the fun."

"Really?" I gripped Aidan's waist and flipped us until I hovered over him. "I believe . . . I will be the one ravishing you."

"I was going to let you." Aidan slid his hand inside my cum soaked jeans. "I want to clean this mess up for you."

"Oh really." I shoved his white shirt up and over his head. "I think I'll feast on you first."

"Thought you needed an agreement between us first." Aidan ran his hand up the back of my shirt and scraped his nails down my spine, causing me to arch into his touch.

"Do, but you blew my mind. I need to repay your kind act."

"Want you to do more than make me explode." Aidan unbuckled my pants, shoving his hand down. "Want to feel this huge rod up my ass, taking me into a new realm of reality."

"Really." I kissed a line between one of Aidan's nipple ring to the other one. "How long these been pierced?"

"Ten years." He arched into my touch as I tugged on the small hoop, gasping as I laved away what had to be a sting.

"You like, pain?"

"Some, babe, some."

My lips sealed over his as my hand explored his bare chest, before I unzipped his pants. I had just gripped his thick, long cock when he was jerked from under me and slammed into the wall.

Before his back hit the wall, my beast came busting from me, landing on two feet, beside a hissing Lord Tang, who held Aidan by his throat. My beast lunged taking Lord Tang down by the knees as the room filled with green haze as a wall of huge Bombaridan surrounded Aidan, who remained stationery and eyes locked on mine. Aidan's hand rested against his neck, but he nodded at me.

Chapter 30

Aidan

"Royal Keeper Aidan, you need to let Commander Theodor know you are well."

Wasn't sure who all had swarmed the room, or how, but I knew they were there to protect Theodor and me. Since my other half was in beast mode, I had to ensure he maintained control.

"I'm fine, babe. Promise."

Theodor's beast walked by Lord Tang, kicking out at the motionless man. Never seen Lord Tang so shocked. Was myself.

"Do you know what set off your leader?"

Theodor's beast came up to my side, rubbing against it and sniffing my crotch.

"Stop that, babe."

The guard that's been asking me questions snorted and rolled his eyes, muttering about how all the Royal Leader became sick puppies when they found their Keeper.

"You had no right to . . ." Lord Tang clambered to his feet, rubbing his kneecap. "You let him take your Clan Leader down."

"You are lucky," I moved so I could see around Theodor and his guard. "That I did not take you down with my claws. You obviously saw my mark on him, which means you are forbidden from interfering. You have complaints with my Inamorato then you come to me. We clear?"

Theodor came up beside me, resting his head against my leg. I dug my fingers into his course thick fur, scratching.

"This . . . This monster has done nothing but disrespect me since he arrived. Me and his Uncle had an agreement. He failed to uphold it."

Theodor roared when Lord Tang jerked my arm up.

"You bare . . . Who the hell put this on you?

Was none of his business. Not like he didn't know. He'd been told who Theodor was to me.

"Who do you think." I jerked my arm back. "Do not man handle me."

"You will not be . . . No. I will not allow it. You gave me your oath."

Damn. Lord Tang had lost his mind if he thought such. He knew the laws. I despised having to remind him of what our laws were, but I would.

"My oath ended the moment I found my Inamorato. You know that." I knelt, taking Theodor's snout in my hands. "I'm ready to go back to your place."

A rich shadow crossed those sexy beast eyes of his, letting me know how sorry he was. Not like I hadn't known when I said it, but it had been worth a shot. Theodor could not leave until things were settled between Connor and Robin.

"See," Lord Tang pointed at Theodor, "he does not wish to take you away from me."

"I promise you," Theodor's guard shook his head, "That is not what that look was for."

"I know it wasn't." I tapped the tip of Theodor's snout. "What he is waiting for has done been resolved."

Bones cracked as Theodor's beast receded. Looked painful. Not just looked felt painful. Had me backing up a bit but I quickly put my arms around him, keeping his from falling.

"What . . . Did . . . You . . . Mean." Theodor's teeth clanked thanks to his fangs still being present.

"Lord Tang . . ." Bobby halted and drew his gun, aiming at the guards and Theodor. "Sir, Connor is gone."

"What!"

The hiss was a roar. Every guard covered their ears, including Theodor. Least I no longer had to reveal that I'd helped Connor and Robin leave the area. Connor knew what him and Robin faced if they stayed. They decided to take matters into their own hands. I'd helped. Not much. Okay, more than I should have, but Lord Tang had no right to keep Connor hidden from his people. Nor did he have the right to hold him hostage.

"Ready?" Theodor wrapped an arm around my waist.

"Yes." I rested my head on his shoulder. "Take me to your place."

"Combatants."

"Commander."

"Home."

Blackness consumed me, making my mind swirl. Bit more intense than when I traveled through air and space, but not much.

Chapter 31

Theodor

I swopped Aidan into my arms, shocked at how light the well-built man was. Aidan's wide eyes and light gasp threw my heart into overdrive as well as my libido. I tossed my head at my General and took the grand staircase two at a time. I was in front of my bedroom door before I put Aidan down.

"Uh . . . Before . . ." Wasn't stalling, but I had to ensure that my Keeper knew the seriousness of his next action.

"I get it." Aidan took his hand and walked us into the bedroom. "We will work out the domestic partnership. Promise."

Chill bumps formed over my skin as Aidan ran his hand up the back of my shirt and around to the front of my jeans.

"Shit."

"What?"

"I was in cum soaked jeans. Yours was unbuttoned."

Aidan chuckled and slipped his hand inside the jeans, coming back out with wet fingers, bringing them up to his mouth. My hips thrust forward when he slipped those digits into his mouth and ran his tongue around them.

"Mmmm . . ."

"Damn, honey."

"The moment you take me, combines our lives for the rest of our lives." Aidan's lips pressed against mine as his hand slipped back into my jeans. He nipped my bottom lip, laving it afterwards. "I cannot wait until we are one."

My hips thrust forward as Aidan's fingers surrounded my hard cock.

"Do you not want us to be one?"

Was all I had to hear. My fingers traced his chest, drifting down his, hard washboard abs. My hands explored the flat surface until I met his jeans. They were unbuttoned and took only a second to push them down his firm hips and thighs.

"Commando."

"Hate the way boxers rides and pinch of underwear so . . ."

Liked him always being bare under his jeans. Sure would save time when I wanted to pull Aidan aside and suck him senseless. From the ten inches straining towards Aidan's stomach, I'd be doing that a lot.

"Got to taste." I dropped to my knees, licking his chest, abs, and hips as I went. "Got to." I ran the flat of my tongue over the tip of the mushroom head.

"Won't be . . . Ah man . . . Won't last . . . Keep it up."

I formed an O with my mouth and swallowed him whole. Took him all the way to the back of my throat. My jaw popped as I widened my mouth and relaxed my throat. Aidan thrust forward once, twice before he groaned and gripped my hair, tugging me away from him.

I pulled my moth from him and looked up. "I'll taste you later." Many times. After all, we had our entire life.

With grace I ran my hands over his thighs and up his hips as I stood, ensuring my jean clad dick brushed over his. I stepped further into Aidan's forcing him back one step at a time. His knees hit the edge of the bed as I tweaked his nipple rings. He thrust his chest forward as he fell backwards.

"Under the pillow."

I stepped back and kicked my shoes off, sliding my jeans down. They went flying behind me with a single kick.

Aidan held up the lube and flipped the lid. "Want me to prep myself?"

Oh man. I'd lose my shit again. Aidan's fingers buried in his ass would send me flying over the top. Again. Not going to happen twice in one night. Ever. My man did not need to think I had no stamina. Next time I blew my load, it would be deep inside my man's ass.

I lifted Aidan and slid him further onto the bed, pushing his legs wide so I could slip between his thighs. My hand covered Aidan's as he passed the lube to me. He lifted his legs and took hold of his knees.

My moth watered at the first sight of my man's hole. He was going to squeeze the life out of me soon as I entered him. Couldn't wait to feel his heat surround me. Least I knew once I was deep inside him, I'd be able to maintain my control longer than I did when he marked me. Then again . . . If he decided to bite while we were making love . . . Shit. I'd have to get use to that. Ensure I did not blow my load before I enjoyed my man.

I squeezed some lube onto my fingers and spread it between his crack, letting my fingers flutter over his pucker. The way it tried to suck the digit in had me forgetting to take it slow and open my man up properly.

Aidan grunted as my entire finger breached him.

"Shit. Sorry, honey."

"It's fine, babe."

His fluttering hot hole squeezed my finger so tight that if my dick had been there it would have been split in half.

"You are fucking tight."

"Been a long while."

Fuck. My cock jerked once, twice. "Good." Was taking all my mental strength not to ask how long, but . . .Wasn't my business, but . . . Not like I expected him to be a virgin. I wasn't. I'd been with someone less than two weeks ago.

"Why's that?"

"Don't like thinking anyone been inside my Keeper."

"More."

"In time."

Aidan's hole squeezed my finger and sucked it in further. "More, please."

"Sure?"

"Yes, babe. Ready."

I slid a second finger in, scissored them a couple of times before a third one in. I pulled them out and placed the tip of my cock against his pucker. It pulsed in time with my throbbing cock.

One glance up and I saw nothing but pure red-blue sparkling eyes. Wasn't sure what it meant, but I could feel the fire seeping down our mental connection and hear Aidan chanting more, more, more.

"Now." Aidan thrust forward. "Please. Need . . . You . . . Get in me." He gripped the base of his cock.

With a short stab the tip of my cock was inside, "Stop me know if you don't want this."

"Never."

I drove in, stopping when my entire head was inside him. Took all my control to hold still as his body adjusted to the invasion. Aidan's face tensed then relaxed as a deep groan slipped from him. A second later, Aidan laid his head back on the pillow and nodded.

"It's us for the rest of our lives."

I went balls deep, pulling back out as fast as I'd bottomed out inside him, thrusting back in just as fast.

"Yes!" Aidan fisted the comforter. "Babe, harder. Harder."

I gripped his hips and yanked Aidan forward while I thrust forward in a slightly angled direction

"Fuck! Yes! More. Faster. Harder. More. Babe, please."

"Tight." I thrust and pulled Aidan forward as fast as I could stand. I was so close to bursting that I could feel my jizz shifting inside my balls. "Perfection."

"Man alive." Aidan lifted his hips and wrapped his hand around his cock. "Won't last . . . Agh . . . Close, babe, close."

I leaned closer, kissing him as I continued to stab my cock deep.

Fuck! Perfect. Stay there.

The mental talk was sexy and all but pushed me over the edge. Better than that was the wetness I felt splashing against my stomach and the walls of Aidan's hole clamped down on me, holding me in place for a moment. Took two more thrust and I was shoving my dick so far into Aidan that I felt my cock swell before it exploded. Cum soaked through my Keeper, sealing us together as one. With the first spurt I felt the full Keeper, Bombardian connection click in. Contentment and building love flowed through me. I hoped to goodness that Aidan felt how much I cared and how deep in love I already was.

"Damn." I rested my head against Aidan's and slowed my breathing. The rise and fall of Aidan's chest and his steady slow breathing lulled me deeper into a state of ease and peace. Before I knew it, my cock slipped free and I laid half over my Keeper.

"Rest, honey." I whispered and took my own advice, tugging Aidan closer to me.

Chapter 32

Theodor

I shot to my feet, snarling and silently summoning my guards. Aidan leapt up, hissing his own disapproval of the intrusion.

"What is - -"

A burly, hairy man appeared in the doorway sporting a machete in one hand and a pistol in the next. Soon as the green mist started forming a bang ricocheted through the room. I jumped in front of Aidan, taking the bullet heading his way. The impact pushed me into Aidan, who caught me, gripping me like the people participating in the trust test.

"Babe. On my God. Babe. Hold on."

My hand, even though it felt like led, rested against Aidan's face, soothing him. The room spun and became filled with blue mist. I heard more shots mix among two long howls and someone ordering my Combatants to tend to their Commander.

"Keeper Aidan, let me to Commander Theodor, please."

I opened my mouth to tell Aidan to let my General to me, but Aidan's face appeared over my head.

"I will take care of my Inamorato." Aidan stared into my eyes, making me curse myself for putting pain in those normal sexy red eyes. "Do you trust me"

I nodded.

"I do not."

Damn. Course my cousins picked up on my need. David, Caleb, and Franklin had arrived and most likely dealt with the intruder swiftly. I should have kept control of how much pain I showed. The shot to my chest had been more of a shock than painful. Wrong. Hurt like a mother, but I'd been through it before. Not to the chest, but . . .

"I don't really care." Aidan hissed. "He is my Inamorato. All I have to have is his trust."'

"David." I went to sit up, but a hand pushed me back down.

"Do not move, you nut." Caleb would be the only one brave enough to call me a name when I was down and out. "Let us take care of you."

"I will take care of him." Aidan shoved Caleb's hand off of me.

"Guys," Franklin's voice gave me a bit of hope that he would try to rein the others in. He did and didn't. "I think . . . Keeper Aidan, if you could enlighten us as to how you can help him that would help."

"He does not have time for that." David snapped. "Earth, I beg your forgiveness for my intrusion . . . "

David pulling on his affinity wasn't shocking. What was, was how fast Aidan acted. Two cool fingers spread across the bullet opening as he lowered his head. Warm lips pressed against my chest, causing my stomach to swirl. Not with bile, but desire so rich I felt my cock try to stir. Might have if I had not felt blood fluttering from the hole in my chest. Little prickles consumed the skin around the entrance room as . . .

Fuck.

Skin stretched, not one bit of pain though, as the bullet jerked free.

"What are you doing?"

All three of my cousins asked, but none tried to stop Aidan. Wasn't sure if they feared my reaction if they laid a hand on my Keeper, or if they were so shocked that they did not think about doing so. Whatever the case, I was glad they didn't. My beast was riled enough. Being shot hadn't bothered it as much as the fact that someone dared shoot my Keeper. I wanted to tear the intruder limb from limb. My cousins had better left some for me. I doubted it, but . . .

"There." Aidan's warm tongue ran across the hole, leaving behind heat worthy of flames we'd conjured last night. "Let me help you sit up."

With a bit a wiggling and Aidan's arms under me, I got into a sitting position. One look around revealed my top five Combatants and my cousins. Course my cousins were covered in blood.

"You three okay?"

"Course." David crossed his arms. "What did he do to you?"

"I" Aidan squeezed my hand, "extracted the bullet and allowed my connection with him to heal him."

"Keeper's can't do that." Franklin crossed his arms.

"He's not a typical Keeper. Remember." Caleb huffed. "Who the hell is after us now?"

Pain rushed over me as my head fell backwards, pulling a grunt and some muttered curses.

"Take it easy, babe. It's healed, but I can't take away the pain."

"Hello."

Aidan whipped his head towards Caleb and hissed, making me laugh.

"He's a Royal Keeper."

David was right. Bryan and Larry were protective of the ones they considered family. They would take on the baddest and vilest monsters if they dared mess with their Bombardian or a friend. Aidan would fit right in with them.

"Did you bother to find out who the asswipe was before you killed him?" I leaned sidewards, expecting to see a pile of torn skin spread across my floor. "Wow. You didn't kill him."

"We aren't total beast." Franklin huffed. "I'll be glad to put him down if you wish, but we won't be able to figure out who he is, who sent him and why."

"I know him." Aidan jerked his pants from the antique chair next to our bed, pulling out his phone.

"Who you calling?" I laid my hand over his.

"Hierarchy Clanman Thomas."

"Who's that?"

"He's over all the Blood Drinkers."

"So . . ." David waved at the man tussled like a pig ready to be put over the fire pit. Right down to the red blood covering his stomach.

Wouldn't have shocked me if David and Caleb split him open, partly. Men could be devious when someone attacked their family. "He's a Blood Drinker."

"Yes. Not a good one either." Aidan locked eyes with me. "He's an Assassin. They are illegal to use. He would not have come after me unless Lord Tang paid him well."

Never thought Lord Tang would go that far. Breaking rules was one thing but hiring a hitman. Then again . . . Lord Tang not only lost one subject to a Bombardian, but his ward. Albeit the ward was human and should have been able to choose who and how he lived his own life without sneaking away.

"I have to report this and then go make sure Lord Tang did not find Connor."

"Robin will keep him safe." I patted Aidan's arm.

The graying red eyes and downward eyes told me that it would take more than words to ease Aidan. His next comment sealed the deal.

"Yes, but . . . It was your cousin . . ."

"Can you reach them?"

Aidan nodded.

"Then use my phone and call them. Tell Robin we will be sending someone to assist him in keeping his Keeper safe."

"You think that is wise?" David propped himself against the wall. "And can you cover up. I've seen way too much of you."

Shit. Hadn't realized I was as naked as Aidan had been. My pants weren't on the chair, so I yanked the blanket off the bed and threw it over me.

"Who's with Bryan?"

"Cain and Tommy."

"How's he doing?"

I asked the question, but kept my ear trained on Aidan's conversation. Whoever he spoke to was not pleased. Plenty of yelling was taking place between the man Aidan called and someone who was there with him. The turn of events had pissed them off. Hierarchy Clanman Thomas did not mince words or take care in how he expressed his feelings. Hardcore and deadly. Me and my cousins had used those words and tone several times and it never ended well for whoever displeased us.

"Medication is working." David twisted his head to Aidan. "Whoever he's speaking to seemed to know quite a bit about us."

Man had asked four times if a Royal Leader had been harmed or if Aidan's Inamorato was safe and if he needed any special healing. That was a part that he did not seemed shocked about. Why though? How did he know of them? Question for Aidan to answer later. First, I had to reassure my cousins that I was fine and that they could go back home. They might not have asked me if I was okay, but three sets of eyes bore into me. More like glared at my chest where the skin was still reddened.

"Don't even go there." David held his hand up when I focused on him. "You two will be coming to my house to stay until you resolve the issue with this tadpole of a Blood Drinker."

"Fuck we are."

"You put me in control."

"While I was gone."

"You are not safe here."

"I have other houses."

"He found you once. He can find you again."

"No. He can't." Aidan laid the phone down. "Hierarchy Clanman Thomas revoked my loyalty pledge to him. He can no longer track where I am or order me to do anything."

Thank god. Still wished I knew such was possible before I brought Aidan back here. I'd inadvertently endangered my cousins and us.

"I did not mean to keep it from you." Aidan nudged my shoulder. 'I'm so use to having it that I did not think of the consequences." He took in a deep breath. "Plus . . . I never through Lord Tang would do something so absurd."

"Doesn't matter." I rested my head on his shoulder. "My cousins are extremely protective over each other. We lost a couple a few months back and it has left us a bit on the cautious side."

"Understandable." Aidan's wink had my cock plumping up. "I personally would not mind meeting the other Keepers."

Wasn't sure if that was a good idea. Didn't want to keep Aidan away from them, but Bryan was expecting twins and he did not need danger in his home, nor have to worry over having a guest.

"It can wait." Aidan slipped an arm around me. "We can go to one of your other homes."

Shit. Forgot that Aidan had an intense mental connection to me. That was going to take some time. I knew that I would feel his distress and emotions, and in some rare cases a Bombardian and Keeper could communicate privately, but . . .

"I don't like that idea." David and Caleb said at once.

"Why not?"

"It is safer and quicker for us to get to you if we are all in one place." David said.

"Caleb and Franklin aren't living with you." Damn. Caleb's huge smile and Franklin's shake of the head had me groaning. "Since when and why?"

"Since you left. We had no idea when, or if, any more Blood Drinkers would show up. You did not tell us much information about what was going on. It was best if we were all together." Caleb shrugged. "Plus, it will help us all know what to expect when we find our Keeper and he becomes pregnant."

"Pregnant!" Aidan's body stiffened.

Agh. Forgot to tell him that might be an issue. Wasn't sure if that came into play with him since he was . . . Hoped it would, but . . .

"On that note," David pushed away from the wall. "I've got to get back to Bryan."

"Oh no you don't." I grabbed hold of David's leg before he could zap himself away. "You started this, and you will stay while . . ." Shit. Not best to have him here why I explained things to Aidan. Was a personal issue and did not need my cousins to know how my Keeper felt about having children. "Fine. Get going."

Not even one second passed before blue mist formed and faded. His Combatants spun on their heels and left the room. My General snatched the Blood Drinker Assassin with him.

Chapter 33

Theodor

Aidan's shoulders shook under my arm. My ass needed kicking. I tugged him onto my lap and wrapped my arms around him, pressing him as close to me as possible.

"I'm fine."

His quavering voice said different.

"You are not." I rested my chin on top of his head. "My cousins . . . Spoke out of turn."

My cousin's ass would be kicked for that. Or it would have been if I hadn't forgotten to enlighten my Keeper. I knew it was a chance, but . . . Then again was it?

"Not really." Aidan's body relaxed into me, nuzzling my neck. Or that's what I wished. Shaking had faded and he'd gone dead still in my arms and against me. "He let something slip that you should have told me."

Couldn't dispute that. Telling Aidan I forgot, wasn't completely true. Then again . . . I had forgotten when we were talking about Keepers. Fact that a Royal Leader could get pregnant was a new concept and not in the typical Bombardian code to their Keeper. Not to mention my mind was full of lust and fever for Aidan. Then again . . . I should not have overlooked such a major aspect.

"I'll let it slide." Aidan nuzzled my neck, pulling a groan from me. "I sort of was in a rush to get my Bombardian into bed. Not to mention I thought I heard it all from Connor's explanation."

"Doesn't apply to Robin and Connor." Might not even to us. After all, far as I knew no other Bombardian paired with a Blood Drinker. "Have you heard of a Blood Drinker being paired with my kind?"

"No." Aidan kissed my chest. "I check with the Hierarchy Clanman soon as I realized who you were to me. He was shocked. So was his secondhand man, my father."

"Why?"

"Lord Tang did not tell them about discovering your kind."

Crap. Me and my cousins would have torn him in half if he kept something like that from us.

"Hold up." I lifted his head from my chest so I could see his sexy blood red eyes. "Did you say your father?"

"Late pick up there, babe."

Oh boy! Wasn't like I thought he came from under a rock, but . . . Had not thought his father would know about me before I met him. Or that I would have been able to tell his father what I was. Human fathers were not told about who their children were paired with. Not because we did not want them to know, but because the law did not allow it. Or yet.

"You aren't sure if this even applies to me, are you?"

"What did your father say?"

"He's was happy for me. Thrilled I found my other half. Going to answer my question?"

"No, honey." I rubbed my head against Aidan's head, soaking in the softness of his baby fine hair.

"Understandable. Far as we know, this kind of pairing has never happened." Aidan sighed. "Although . . . Something Hierarchy Clanman Thomas said made me think he's found out more about this."

"What was that?"

"Something about people forgetting to clue him in sucked balls."

I couldn't refrain from chuckling.

"His words, not mine."

"He didn't say anything else about it?"

Aidan shook his head. "He's not one to share facts with people he considers commoners."

Commoners? Oh boy. Some leaders were pricks. "Would he talk to me?"

"Not sure. I can ask my father, if you want."

"Might. Let me talk to my cousins first."

"How come a Royal Keeper can get pregnant, when a typical Keeper can't?"

I rotated my neck a couple of times then pressed a light kiss to Aidan's head. "Our blood is different. Royal Leaders carry more of Edward Lincoln's genes."

"Who's he?"

"First Bombardian."

"What makes your blood different?"

"The Type W gene." I gave him a small squeeze as he leaned back, placing his hands on the floor beside my knees.

"Does all Bombardians not carry the gene?"

"No. We are not sure why it faded in some and not in others. Each Bombardian is checked upon birth. Those who carry any amount of the gene is put on the royal blood list. The ones with the most goes on top and is the next one in line to take a Royal Leader's seat when the time comes. It's rare to shift from one family to the next. Any child born to a Royal Leader carries the most royal blood."

"You think it's a . . . Protection of some kind to keep the family line in power?"

"Might be. Not sure though. We just recently found out it was possible."

"How come?"

"Years back there was what is referred to as The Awakening. It is where the Bombaridans and royal blood carries were told that three Royal Leaders had been killed. David, Caleb, and me were still young. Our fathers took over for us until we became of age, then they stepped aside. Far as we knew no Royal Leader had ever found a Keeper. In fact, we were taught that we had to have a child in case we never found our Protector. David rebelled on this for years. In fact, he only attempted once to be with a woman. He couldn't do it. He swore he had a Keeper." No one believed him and his family had rounds with him about his stubbornness. "When he ran into Bryan . . . Well, let's just say it was a huge shock to us all. It was right before his Pledging Ceremony that we discovered that those three Royal Leader who we thought died were alive and living in seclusion with their Keepers. They'd remained hidden from their own kind to avoid disgrace coming to the Royal Leaders who led at the time."

"Why?"

"We are a majority rules society and there was only two that decided to kick the other three Royal Leader aside. It was there way of protecting our kind. Soon as they found out David found a Keeper; they came seeking me."

"Why you?"

"I'm the eldest, so I lead all the meetings and run all the votes. Basically, I . . ."

"You control what takes place among the Royal Leaders until a vote is required. Right down to putting someone else in charge."

I nodded and ran my hand up his flat stomach, stopping to pinch his nipples.

"How long has your family been in power?"

"All the way back to start of our race."

"So . . . This royal blood is stronger in the current leaders, which is why you were required to have children."

Another nod and another pinch of his nipples, getting a moan from him.

"Doesn't explain how I might be able to get pregnant?"

"We aren't really sure. All we know is that when David found Bryan and the three that were exiled revealed their selves to us, they told us they had children. Shocked the shit out of us, but we were so focused on David's Pledging Ceremony and the pending attack that was at our doorstep that we all forgot it was a possibility. Came slamming back when Bryan started being so sick."

Aidan arched his back into my palm as I rubbed it across his jean clad dick. "You want us to have children?"

Would my answer please him? Upset him? Didn't matter. I would not lie to him. "I've tried since I took the Royal Leader seat."

"You have?" Aidan's face scrunched up. "How?"

"I'm sure you know how children are made."

"Yes, but . . ." Aidan brushed my hand away from his cock. "We are paired up. Surely you weren't matched with a male when you prefer women."

"I do not prefer women, but . . . Had no problem sleeping with them to reach my goal." Had been drilled into me that my preference did not matter. I had two jobs. Run the Bombardians and produce the next leader.

"What does . . ." Aidan's head went back and forth, and his rich blood red eyes went gray as his lips turned down. "I won't be able to allow you to . . . You are my Inamorato. You should . . . No. I won't be able to let you go to a woman to gain a child. It's just not . . ."

Aidan's words were not understandable. He was hissing so loud my beast roared. Partly because his ears hurt and because his Keeper was pissed. I done the only thing I could think of, pressed in on him until his back hit the floor. I thrust my cock against his jean covered one, letting him feel just how much I longed to make love to him.

"Shh. I will not be going to anyone else." I rubbed my groin against his. "My cock belongs inside your body. No one else."

Aidan pressed up into me, sealing his lips over me, shoving his tongue through them, taking my mouth in the most primal manner. I laid there and let him take what he needed. Reassure himself that his Bombardian had feelings only for him. Wasn't sure how long we laid there kissing and rutting, didn't matter, what did was that the two of us were on the same page about that concept. All that was left was to find out if Aidan would give him a child. If not . . . My family would cease to belong to the Royal Leaders. I was an only child and none of my cousins bore royal blood. Another reason my father insisted I have a child. He wanted multiple grandchildren.

"I can feel your . . ."

I placed a finger over Aidan's mouth. "I promise I will go to no one else from here out."

"I know." Aidan wiggled so he laid beside me. "I was going to say, that we could always get a surrogate."

"Might not have to."

"How will we know?"

"I think . . . I'm not sure, but I believe this Hierarchy Clanman Thomas knows about another pairing like ours."

"I'm sure my father will call me soon. Hierarchy Clanman Thomas wanted to speak with the Assassin."

"Least my cousins didn't kill him. I would have."

"I know. I would have if you hadn't been shot."

"Do you think they will tell you?"

"They will not want me going into a relationship blind."

We'd done enough talking. It'd been too long since I felt my Keeper surrounding me. Then again . . . I'd not had time to explore his hot body. I let my hand unsnap his jeans and shoved them down his hip. Aidan gasped and lifted his hips for me. He spread his legs and let me snuggle between his legs. I traced his lower lip with my tongue as I threw his jeans onto the bed. I licked a path from his lip, over his chin, down his neck, over to the right dark nipple then sucked it into my mouth, teething it.

"Fuck!"

Sensitive? Us having a private chatting link was going to be nice.

I like talking to you this way.

Me to. I switched to the other nipple and rolled it between my teeth until Aidan moaned.

We going to your cousin's house?

I licked a path down over his abs, pausing to swirl my tongue around his belly button before I dropped to the dark brown curls trying to hide his treasure.

Later. Much later, honey.

I sucked him in all the way down my throat, silencing him and taking all thoughts from him.

Chapter 34

Theodor

After three more rounds of hot and intense lovemaking I packed a couple of bags and zapped us to David's house, only to find it empty. I stood in the center of the living room, scratching my head as Aidan walked around taking in each photo and trinket David and Bryan had.

"Thought you said they were expecting us."

"He is." What was going on?

I pulled my phone from my back pocket when Cain popped in, baring his stern, no one messes with my Commander and gets by with it.

"What happened, General?"

"Someone showed up here right after you talked to Commander David."

"Who?" Aidan spun taking two steps back.

You okay, honey?

His eyes hold murder in them. It's taking all my control not to protect myself.

There is no need in that. He would not harm you but give me a second and you'll be able to come to me. Will that help?

Please. I don't want to cause trouble and . . .

Didn't need anything else said. I would not let my Keeper be distressed in any manner. I knew what it felt like to stare into Cain's eyes when someone messed with David. The two of them had been best friends and Cain was the most driven General any of them had ever had. He could intimidate the strongest willed man.

"Move to the side, General."

Cain did not wait for an explanation he simply did as told and bowed his head when I held my hand out to Aidan.

"Sorry, Commander Theodor, did not mean to spook your Keeper."

"It's fine."

Aidan came to me and pressed himself into my side, letting his hand slip into my back pocket.

I knew you were big. So were lots of those . . . What did you call those guys who came to protect you?

Combatants.

Right. But . . . Damn, he's bigger than any of them. I'm not sure I could take him if I had to defend us.

You would not have to do so from him. He would die for either of us.

Yours did not look that big.

He is the biggest and baddest Combatant we've had in generations. David is a lucky guy to have him as a General and as a best friend.

Are all his Combatants that big?

Yes.

Wasn't sure why David had so many huge Bombardians as Combatants, but I knew very few chose to mess with him. Or they hadn't until he found his Keeper. Since then . . . Life for all of us had been . . . Dangerous. David more than anyone of us.

Many threats did not come my way, but I had people always coming to me to solve issues. I had a great team of Combatants and would not trade them for anyone, besides maybe Cain. But he would never leave David's side. Not that me and Cain would get along. He is the type of General who takes his job of protection as a way of life and no one came between him and protecting his Commander. I did not want a guard that intense. I liked to solve my own issues and my General knew me well enough to know when to stand back and let me and when to step in and take control.

"Where did David take everyone."

"Influence Manner."

"Why in the world . . . How did he . . ."

"Said you'd be confused." Cain held his hand up when I snarled at him. "No offense meant, Commander Theodor."

Confused . . . Ah shit.

"David put you up to that." Course he had. David and his other cousins were jousters in their own way. "Where did he really go?" There was no way David took them to Influence Manner. That was my second backup home and no one, but me could enter. Unless . . . "Did that little shit pull on my affinity?"

Cain took two large steps back then knelt.

"He did. Didn't he."

Cain's silence was answer.

"You are free to go." I snorted as Cain popped out. "My cousin is a big shit head."

"Shit head?" Aidan looked up at me with confusion.

"He tapped into Fire and gained access to my second backup home."

"How did he manage that?" Aidan stepped out of my arms. "I thought you said all your places were secure."

"They are."

"Then how did he know how to get into your place?"

David was the smartest dumbass among the Royal Leaders. Each cousin had their own skill set, like each Bombardians, but David's was special and rare. In reality, David was stronger than me and should lead the Royal Leader, but he had come into his role a few years later than me, making me the eldest.

"I think it might not be safe for us to go to another place of yours."

"Why?" I walked around the living room, hunting for anything that might be out of place. Was sure David had Cain search the house soon as the intruders had been dealt with. But doing one of my own eased my raging beast. Not that it should matter. Aidan had never been in David's house. Lord Tang . . .

Crap. Lord Tang had invaded David's house after his goons had been captured. Lord Tang had a mental connection to the Bombardians he enlisted to aid him. Damn it. I needed my ass kick.

David should have left the home the moment I realized who was in charge of the invasion. Why had I not? Was I so distracted by the fact that Lord Tang broke his promise that my mind slipped? Then my mind had went to tracking him down, then unraveling the Marked One's mystery and then I found . . . The best person in my life.

"Hey," Aidan gripped my chin and tugged my head down to him. "You are only a Bombardian and was juggling more than one should. You might have made an oversight, but I am sure your cousins are holding no grudge."

"He's right." David's voice had me spinning around, cursing for not knowing he was there.

"Sorry, Theodor." David winked at me. "Cain said you looked a bit unpleased with me."

"Am."

"Seems like you are beating yourself up over something that we all should have considered."

"Me more than you."

"Why's that?" David moved over to the sofa and sat.

"I'm the eldest."

David's wide eyes told me all I needed to know. My voice came across weak as the excuse was. I should have known my cousins would pick up on it. Any of them would have. Lameness was not tolerated among us and I knew it better than any of us. There was no reason for me to try to justify my feelings.

"Why did you use my affinity to get into my house?"

"That wasn't kind." Aidan moved in front of David and pointed at him. "Rude in fact."

"Shit." David ran a hand over his face. "Another smarty pants Keeper."

"Bryan and Larry will love him." I yanked Aidan back against me. "I sure do."

"Okay." David stood. "Then let's get out of here before my home is invaded a second time in one day."

"I've not forgot your stunt." I wrapped an arm around Aidan and zapped us from David's.

Chapter 35

Aidan

Soon as my feet were once again on a solid surface my mind began replaying all the stunts that Lord Tang had played over the years. There'd been several, which I kept all from the Hierarchy Clanman Thomas. I'd not told my father either because none of them broke any laws. Not even when he took in Connor. Most thought he took Connor in and raised him because he was the last of his family, but that hadn't been the truth. Connor was the last living relative that Lord Tang had. He'd kept a watch over his family since he decided to become a Blood Drinker. Such acts aren't allowed anymore, but two centuries ago it was common practice. Lord Tang had five children in all. Two by a wife and three by a mistress. He'd consented to the change after a huge battle left him with a piece of a wagon in his gut. He would have died from his injuries if his maker had not offered him life. He knew then he'd have to leave his family, which bothered him, but his maker told him he could watch them from afar. It became an obsession. Not one the Hierarchy Clanman would have allowed if he knew. Watching over your human family wasn't unlawful, but it was frowned upon for that very reason. Taking Connor into the domain was another skirting of the laws. I might have been wrong to keep his escapades a secret, but . . . What I did was done. No changing it. Wasn't my fault that Lord Tang had chosen to break the laws. All I could do was report him and leave it up to my father to deliver punishment on him. If my father had the chance. If Theodor and his cousins get their hands on him first. . . There'd be nothing left for my father to deal with.

"Honey?"

I squeezed Theodor's side and grinned up at him. "Introduce me."

Theodor waved at the light blue sofa and the young man stretched out on it. Man looked pale and held his stomach like it was about to rebel on him. Wasn't difficult to figure out who that was. From what Theodor had said, Bryan had been sick since he became pregnant.

"That's Bryan."

Bryan lifted a hand and waved, grinning. "Nice to meet you."

"You to. Hope all is well."

"Going great."

"Right." A tall dark-haired man said. "My great niece and nephew are giving him a fit today."

"Hey," Theodor walked over to the man sitting at a desk and yanked the seat back. "How did you get on my computer?"

"Hacked it." The broad shoulder man shrugged and scooted back up to the desk.

"Damn it." Theodor's words trailed off into a loud ear-piercing howl, which had Bryan leaping to his feet and a sapling appeared in the middle of the room.

"Damn it, Bryan." Theodor's tone held no sharpness or anger, simple frustrations. Not at Bryan, but himself for losing control.

"Neat." I walked up to the small tree and ran my fingers across the top. "How did you do that?" Was interesting that someone could produce such beauty so quick and without any outward sign, other than leaping. My curiosity also gave Theodor time to settle his beast.

Thanks, honey.

What I'm here for.

More than that, honey.

I know, babe.

Bryan's hand rested over his heart as he glared at Theodor. "What the heck were you thinking?"

"That this is my home. It has done been breeched by David and my other crazy cousin hacked my computer."

My distraction didn't work as I hoped, so I walked over to him and pressed myself against him. I ran my hand up the back of his shirt, getting skin contact. He slumped into my touch.

That's it, babe, calm down.

"Bryan," David stared at the tree, "what did Theodor do to piss you off. He's just got here."

"Scared me to death."

"Why?"

"I howled in my own damn house." His arm wrapped around my waist and he marched us into the hallway.

"You okay, babe?"

"Yes." His heaving chest told otherwise. "Need a few minutes away from everyone."

Seemed to be a lot of tension flowing through his other half. Not what I expected. Theodor spoke highly of his cousins and their relationship. He'd never given me a detailed description of how the Royal Leaders worked, but I'd felt the deep connection and respect he held for his cousins. They worked as a unit. More like brothers than cousins. They joked with one another and fought for one another. Him being so up in the air with his cousin didn't seem right. Had I been wrong?

"I thought you all got along."

"We do."

"Don't seem like it."

"Normally, their stunts don't bother me."

Chapter 36

Theodor

What had me upset? My cousins always joked around. It's how we dealt with life. How we handled every meeting. David breaking into my place and Franklin into my computer was mild actions compared to some of our tactics in the past. So why . . .

"Are they trying to pay you back for your treatment of them?"

"Partly. Doesn't bother me." I leaned against the hallway, cursing myself for painting the hallway some neon yellow. "I hate this color."

"Good."

"You going to remodel this place?"

"I was hoping to convince you to change this part."

"Honey, you can redo anything you want in any of our homes."

"I can?" Aidan pressed his chest into mine, letting his cock brush mine.

I let my head rest in the grove of his neck. "I'd give you the world."

"Even if I can't give you a child?"

"Of course."

Aidan's lips slammed over mine as he rubbed his dick over mine. *Got a bedroom here?*

Seven of them.

Umm . . .

Aidan sucked my lower lip between his teeth, nipping. "Take me to . . . On second thought." He dropped to his knees and unzipped my pants. "I'll just . . ."

Hot, wet moist lips wrapped around my hardening cock. He took me all the way down his throat, taking every inch of me, sucking as his tongue ran across the underside of my cock.

"Damn, honey." Every muscle in my body relaxed and my knees threatened to buckle. "Yes . . ."

"Shit."

Franklin's voice had my eyes popping open. "Leave."

Franklin left muttering about how he could not get away from sex-fiend men if he tried. Before I figured out what he meant, Aidan's fingers brushed across my balls, tickling until my entire body soared with desire.

"Keep that up . . . Damn . . . Don't stop."

Aidan's mouth knew exactly what to do and where and how much pressure to apply while he deep throated me. Electric currents zinged over my entire body, drawing loud moans from me. When Aidan's tongue swirled around the mushroom head, stopping to dip into the slit my breath left my body. Explosion clung to the edge of my mind, soul, and body, but was right out of reach until . . .

A light squeeze of my balls had me falling over the edge and shouting.

"Aidan!"

Each swallow Aidan took increased the enticing ripples washing over me. My Keeper didn't let a drop slip from his mouth and made sure to lick my cock clean before he pulled off. Soon as he released me, I tugged on his hair, bringing him up so I could taste each corner of his mouth.

"Amazing." I muttered against Aidan's lips as I reached down and cupped him, finding a wet spot.

"Got some sweats I can wear?"

I nodded, tugging him up the stairs. "We have to find some way for you to get your stuff."

"I'll ask my father to retrieve my stuff for me, if it's okay for him to bring it to me."

"Should be, but I'll check with the others. I also think it might be the best time to ask if this Thomas guy could tell you what he has discovered since the first time you discussed our pairing with him."

"Want to shower before you change?"

"You going to join me?"

"Need to speak with my cousins. Am I able to fill them in on where we stand with Lord Tang and what we know and about Hierarchy Clanman Thomas?"

"Don't see why not."

"Join us when you are done." I kissed him and pointed to the bathroom door. "There's six shower heads, so enjoy." I left him smiling and walking into the bathroom.

"Oh, babe."

I paused in the doorway, looking back over my shoulder.

"You taste amazing and your balls fit perfect in my hand."

I was across the room, cupping him as I licked the spot between his shoulder and neck.

"Your ass clings to my cock just like it knows who it belongs to."

"It does."

"Did I please you?"

"More than."

I let my hand slip into the back of his pants, brushing over his hole, getting a groan and thrust back from Aidan.

"Then I pleased you a second ago?"

"I'll show you how much later." I dipped my finger in his hole for a second.

"Give me a preview."

I turned him around and pushed him over the cabinet. "Stay there." I had his pants around his ankles in a second, spreading his cheek as my tongue ran through the folds, pausing to flick his pucker. Aidan's leg gave, causing me to grab his hips to keep him upright.

Like that?

"Love it." A deep moan slipped from Aidan. "More. Please. Babe. More."

I dipped the tip of my tongue in. His hole sucked me in. I shook my head to the side, letting Aidan's ass take more of me as I slipped a finger in under my tongue.

"Fuck, babe." Aidan's hand fisted his cock.

I knocked his hand away and took hold of him, tight. I ran my finger over the tip, gathering his pre-cum to ease my motion. Took only three stokes before Aidan was shooting his load over the cabinet door.

"Too tired to shower." Aidan's leg gave way and I scooped him into my arms, carrying him to the bed, letting his pants fall along the way.

"Rest, honey."

"Got to . . ." Aidan's eyes fell shut and his breathing slowed.

I spread the 'Together Forever' marriage blanket my grandmother had made me. It was the first time it'd been used. Until David found his Keeper. It had been kept in my closet in the far corner. I'd dug it out the night after David found Bryan. Looked as if it had truly brought me good luck. My grandmother told me it would. Would I have found Aidan earlier if I'd kept it on the foot of my bed? Didn't matter. Had him now and it was time I found a way to solve the issue with Lord Tang. I kissed the top of Aidan's head and then left.

Chapter 37

Theodor

Bryan was sitting up when I walked into the living room. "They are in the conference room." He picked up a glass and sipped from it.

Should have looked there first, but . . . "What are you watching?"

"Don sent it to me."

Blood ooze from someone's round stomach. Gross. "What is that?"

"The birth of his first son."

Shivers raced over my entire body. How in the world . . . Knew the procedure for a man giving birth would be . . . Had not considered a Keeper having to have their stomach sliced open. Damn. What a Keeper went through to have a child. I would make sure Aidan saw the video. Only after he was expecting. Sight might scare the shit out of him.

"You going to be okay?"

I nodded.

"David went whiter than you."

Bet he did. The mere thought turned my stomach and made me thankful that I was not the one going through it.

"Told him he had to be in the room the entire time."

"You didn't."

"He did." David tapped my shoulder. "Going to join us?"

I shook my head and followed him down the hallway.

* * *

"He's here." Caleb smiled then laughed, rubbing his neck. "Looks like your Keeper had some major fun."

I glanced in the mirrored wall. Shit. Three dark red circles graced the left side of my neck. Not to mention a set of fang marks. I knew Aidan fed, but had not considered the fact that there would be marks.

Didn't bother me. Really. What I needed to know was the consequences of such. What I needed to do to remain healthy, if anything. Would Aidan know? Would it be different than a Blood Drinker or human? Sure it would be.

"So . . ." Franklin leaned back in his chair, propping his foot on the solid oak conference table. "What are we going to do about this Blood Drinker thing?"

"What!" My throat stung as the growl rippled up and out of it.

Franklin held his hand up. "Did not mean your Keeper."

"Then what?"

"He was addressing," David took a seat and waved me to the table. "He was talking about the one, or ones, that keep invading our homes."

Right. Lord Tang. Two invasions. David's main house. My second home. Intrusions wasn't something Royal Leaders needed. Bryan being pregnant only increased our need to keep the unknown and unwanted from our homes. Perceived danger would send David into full beast mode. Not something we needed. Bombardians expected their leaders to control their beast and keep their heads on straight. Not an easy feat when your Keeper was in danger. Even worse since Bryan was expecting twins.

"What has Royal Keeper Aidan said about Lord Tang?" Caleb crossed his arms.

"You know he called a head guy, who sent someone to retrieve the Assassin. That was the second time he called him."

"When was the first?" Franklin stared me right in the eyes.

"Right after he discovered I was his other half."

"What was he told then?" David asked.

"At that time the guy said he'd never heard about such a pairing but ensured him that no one could forbid him from taking care of his other half."

"At that time?" Caleb raised an eyebrow.

"When he called him back, the guy talked different. Aidan is going to call him again and see what has changed. If anything."

"You think he will be honest with you?"

My beast roared, but I forced him into the background. My cousins had the right to ask their questions. To even wonder if Aidan would tell them anything about his kind. It might ruffle my beast's fur, but . . .

"Will you," Caleb sat forward, resting his elbows on the table. "Allow us to ask him some questions?"

Didn't like the idea but understood where Caleb was coming from. Would Aidan understand? I hoped so. The more they knew about Blood Drinkers and what they knew about them and how they knew about them and what a pairing such as theirs meant. Bombardians had to know what to expect. The facts had to be told to all Bombardians, and that would come from their leaders.

"Babe," Aidan stood in the doorway, wearing only his jeans. "It is not an interrogation."

I licked my lips. Wasn't sure if I salivated over my Keeper or what. All I knew was that I remained still. Racing over and claiming Aidan's lips and carrying him back to the bedroom, fucking him hard and fast, had to wait.

"Damn, cousin." David waved his hand in front of his face. "Think you are worse than me."

"Think so." Caleb sighed.

"Now he is." Franklin coughed. "Least I never caught you getting a BJ in a hallway."

"Hey," Theodor motioned Aidan to my side. "It is my house. I can get a blowjob anywhere I want."

"True." David went to the fridge and got a bottle of water, holding it up.

"Get me one." Franklin caught the bottle David tossed him.

"Anyone else?"

I looked over at Aidan, who shook his head. "You sure . . . I do not want you to do . . . If you aren't comfortable, or it will get you in trouble, I don't want you to . . ."

"It won't." Aidan rested his head against my shoulder as I slipped my arm around his waist. "I can most likely get Hierarchy Clanman Thomas to speak with you directly."

"Think so?" David downed his water in one gulp.

Aidan nodded. "He's a great guy. Levelheaded. Tries to keep each Blood Drinker inline."

"How does he manage that?" Franklin sat his water down. "He's only one person."

"There are not many of my kind left."

"What's that mean?" David tossed his bottle across the room into the recycling bin.

"Only ten clans left in the US."

Sounded like a small amount, but . . . "How man in each clan?"

"No more than twenty in those. Lord Tang has about forty. He's the largest clan."

Overall small numbers. There were at least two thousand Bombardians in the US. More than a thousand in five other countries. "How many overseas?"

"About a thousand in France Double that in Canada. Those areas have their own leaders, though."

Explained how Hierarchy Clanman Thomas handled everyone. Royal Leaders made the laws for all Bombaridans in the US. We had people that worked for us to research the issues that arose and to enforce our rulings. There was no one single leader. We voted and majority ruled.

"How long you been around?" I scooted closer to him.

"I'm four hundred."

Damn. Had not considered that Aidan might be older than me. Then again . . . I had not taken time to get to know the basic relationship information. Simply believed Aidan would fill me in at some point. My trust had been well placed.

"Lord Tang isn't but a couple decades older than me." Aidan sucked his lower lip between his lips, making my cock jump.

Keep that up and I'll fuck you right here in front of them. I winked at Aidan when he smiled.

Exhibitionist. Neat.

Not really. You just drive me wild and seeing you suck that lip only makes me want your hot wet mouth around my cock until I explode down your throat. My cock was at full mask and needed its man.

This is important. Hold that thought. Aidan moved his chair closer to mine. "Hierarchy Clannman Thomas is the strongest. He has bested every challenge that came his way over the last four hundred years. I was told he was the second person to hold the seat."

Other words . . . He was older than Aidan and he had no idea how much.

"You want privacy while you talked to your leader?" David sprang to his feet and rushed out the door before I even picked up on a massive green cloud mist invading my house. My General appeared at my side with the rest of my Combatants and told Aidan to stay put. Did not wait to see if Franklin and Caleb followed. I knew they would be on my heels. What I didn't know was what set David off. Quickly found out.

Snarls and growled. Clanking teeth greeted me as I reached the living room. David was in beast form and fending off Lord Tang, who kept hissing and swinging his clawed hands. Ten other Blood Drinker engaged in a fight with David's Combatants. Cain and two others formed a circle around Bryan, who held his stomach tight.

"Commander Theodor," my General appeared at my side. "What do I do?"

"Protect Aidan. The rest . . ." I threw my hands forward and charged into the midst of the battle.

I dropped the veil I kept over my beast and accepted the slight stinging that a rushed shift created. Seconds later I stood behind Lord Tang. Thought I had the drop on him, but the next time he struck at David he continued around, lashing at me. David used the split second of reprieve to lung for Lord Tang's knees. His jaws clinched around Lord Tang's legs.

Lord Tang threw his head back, hissing and thrashing his arms. A hint of metallic filled the air, driving my beast into motion. Perfect opportunity for my beast to act. It latched his teeth around the back of Lord Tang's neck. Lord Tang kicked his legs back, striking my hind legs. The contact might have sent me to the ground, if my beast had not been holding tightly to Lord Tang's neck. Did make me tighten my hold, but I made sure not to break his neck. Lord Tang reached over his shoulder, driving his claws into my beast's shoulder. Blood seeped down my shoulder and over my front leg, but I kept hold of his neck. David dug his teeth deeper into the man's legs until he crumpled to the floor, screaming and kicking. My jaws ached from the tight hold I had on him. Before I could get him to submit another beast sunk their teeth over one of his arms as another one grasped his other arm. The four of us held him in place. The Blood Drinker refused to give up. He kept right on thrashing and struggling to free himself. Several pieces of my furniture were knocked down and smashed. Not sure if he would have given up, if . . .

"Freeze."

There was no shouting. Simple a booming voice that brought Lord Tang to a halt.

Chapter 38

Aidan

"I will be fine." I snapped at the brute standing in front of me. "Go help Theodor."

The man gave me a slight nod, snapping his finger. He faded into nothingness as another large man appeared behind me. The first man wasn't gone long until he popped back in front of me. He pointed at the man behind me and he faded into nothingness as well.

"Why are you standing here?"

"I have my orders."

Course he did. I had my as well. Or my ingrained protective streak. I yanked my phone from my pocket and pressed one. It rang twice and my father picked up.

"Lord Tang has either sent someone else or came himself."

"What are you doing?"

What did the brute think I was doing? I knew Theodor did not want me in the fray. Left me one option. He might hate me for calling in the one man that could bring Lord Tang to a halt, but . . . I had a responsibility just like he did.

"You going to answer me?"

I shook my head at the man in front of me.

"Okay."

The line went dead. Just like my father. One word and then all action. The loud snarls and growls told me there were more than one beast in action. Not that I didn't understand. David had to protect his family. There was no way he would stand by and allow danger to approach his Keeper. His reaction would be worse since his Keeper was expecting twins.

There was nothing harming me. Lord Tang would not come after me. Nope. He was after the one who took his subjects. The one in charge of the one that took Connor from him. Nope. I was not the threat . . . Then again . . . He had tried to kill me. Didn't matter. I could not sit around and wait like some invalid. I was up and heading for the door when the guard blocked my path. My knees went as my fist did. One two hit. Stomach and nose. Blood flowed and he doubled over, giving me the perfect opportunity to side step him.

Chapter 39

Theodor

Thumps radiated around the room as Lord Tang's eye closed and he went motionless. I kept hold of him. Would not let him go until I heard the cracking of bone. Not to mention I felt fire zipping over my body as David pulled on both of our affinity to aid his second fast shift. There was no way I was going to release Lord Tang until I knew David was full human.

"You can release him."

I shook my head, making Lord Tang's head move side to side.

"He will not until you explain who you are and how you managed to get inside." David's neck popped as he shoved the lingering effects of the fast shift away.

"David," I turned my head towards the sound of my Keeper. *What are you doing in here?* I loved the mental connection that I had with Aidan.

I had to come.

I put guards with you for a reason.

I know babe, but . . . This is Hierarchy Clanman Thomas.

How did he know to show up?

I called him when I heard the fight.

Why?

He could gain control of Lord Tang and his small army. Keep you from getting hurt.

I would have sighed if I could. I knew my Keeper done right, but still . . . The third invasion of one of the Royal Leader's home meant our protection skill did not work well against the Blood Drinkers. Looked as if we had to come up with a way to keep them out. Or the ones we wanted to remain away. I hated that I brought trouble here while Bryan was in residence. Not to mention my own Keeper. I expected some retaliation from Lord Tang, just not . . . Two fast attacks . . . Unexpected.

"I take it you know this man." David's voice pulled me back to the matter at hand. Rest would be addressed among me and my cousins after this was over.

"Yes." Aidan came into the room with my General following. If the man hadn't been frowning, holding his stomach and blood flowing from his nose, I might have ripped into him once I made sure Lord Tang was no threat.

Lord Tang remained motionless, which had me releasing my hold, letting him drop to the floor. I shook my head and then double checked that Lord Tang was out of it. With a tentative pace I made my way over to Aidan. Didn't let my beast go to the back. In beast mode I could protect Aidan better. Not to mention did not dare pull on my affinity so close as David had. It would leave me vulnerable. Not that it mattered. My three cousins would not let anything happen to me.

"How did you get in here?" David stepped over Lord Tang's prone motionless body.

"I will tell you all what you need to know soon as I deal with Lord Tang and his disrespect to you and your family."

I nudged Aidan's leg and walked up to David.

David looked down, nodding twice and motioned Caleb forward. "How do you plan on doing that?"

"I will escort him to our prison. Along with his followers."

Aidan's gasp drew a loud snarl from my beast.

"Not your Royal Keeper, Commander Theodor."

He knew how to address me. Meant . . . Our thoughts were right. Some point between the first contact Aidan had with him and the second call, he had discovered more about Bombardians. How? Who spilled facts?

"Aidan," Hierarchy Clanman Thomas shifted to the left, and I followed him, keeping my self between the still perceived enemy and my Keeper. "I appreciate your call."

"My pleasure." Aidan stood behind me, letting his hand brush across my beast's back. "Yet, I do not believe that all of my former Clan deserves prison time. They simply follow Lord Tang out of fear."

"I did not mean the entire clan."

My beast sat down, letting Aidan's soothing touch ease the fire racing over me. My beast was gathering up his affinity, readying itself for any threat that returned to its family.

"I was hoping you would consider taking over the clan."

"No."

Solid firm no showed me my Keeper knew me. I would not have kept him from doing so, if that's what he wanted. Didn't mean I would have liked for my Keeper to have such a position. Took a large amount of time to lead. Not to mention it put him in a state of danger. Not something my beast would have liked.

"May I ask why."

"Simple. My Inamorato has been found and it is my job to ensure his safety."

My safety?

"I believe he can keep himself safe."

I could.

"I do not. Will not put myself in a position that would cause him more concern and fear. It would not be wise or helpful to him. As his Keeper it is my job to keep him calm. And at this point and time it is more important I stay at his side."

Love. Happiness. Pleasure. Desire. Above all else, ease. Rushed through me. Didn't even matter that the others in the room could pick up on my desire for my Keeper. No Bombardian could ask for more from their Keeper. He not only answered the question, but he did so without giving away more information about the Bombardians than he needed to. As much as I hated admitting it to myself, or my cousins, the Royal Leaders found themselves in a state of upheaval. Last few days had been very stressful. Not only with Bombardians, but also with the fact that Larry was about to go in front of the world and announce us to all the humans. Not to mention that the last few months had showed us just how many enemies we have among our own people. More would come from the humans. Some of them would believe us and leave us alone, but we knew some would come at us in many different ways. We had to be ready and able to handle all of those.

"Acceptable." Hierarchy Clanman Thomas came up to Lord Tang's motionless body.

"What did you do to him?"

David's voice wavered, like it did when he was exhausted from pulling on an affinity. I needed to shift and give him a reprieve. David's double usage of affinities and the fact that he pulled on Fire twice in one day left him exhausted.

"I put him to sleep."

Those words soothed my beast and gave me the prefect time to take control of my beast and send him back.

"What is he doing?"

"Shifting back." Aidan moved so he stood a foot from me. His guards moved with him. "Give him a few minutes."

David, Caleb, and Franklin moved to stand behind me. There was no way they would leave me vulnerable while there a possible threat loomed. Lord Tang might have been sleeping, but his other goons were wide awake. Motionless, but awake and could attack.

"There is no need for such actions. I would not harm a Bombardians." Hierarchy Clanman Thomas took three steps back. "But I understand your unease."

"How come?" Aidan glanced down at me as I shook away the lingering mind fuzziness.

"There has been peace among the Blood Drinkers since the first Royal Leader was formed."

"How come you did not tell Aidan this when he first contacted you?" I stood, thanking goodness that we shifted back with the clothes we had on to start with.

"I was not aware of it at that time."

"Neither were we." I wrapped my arm around Aidan's waist. "Until my Uncle was attacked by one of Lord Tang's Blood Drinkers none of us knew about your kind."

"I am not sure why I was not told or why you were not."

Meant there were more facts, important ones, buried over the years. Least it did not just happen to me. Not a good thing. Every fact was supposed to be written down, giving each new leader the hardcore truth among the world they lived among. There was no way for me to know who had failed to write down. One thing was clear, whoever had was long gone from this world.

"What does this agreement state?" I took a second to take in the upside-down coffee table. The shattered end table and the shredded sofa and chair. Long claw marks ran down the new flat screen TV. Cords danged from where the scone lights beside the fireplace had hung. Overall, there was less damage than I expected.

"No Blood Drinker is to attack or interfere in your way of life. In return, your kind will respect our privacy and refrain from outing us to the humans."

Basic agreement. One that should have been easy to follow, but Lord Tang broke the peace the moment he sent Bombardians to attack. That gave the Bombardians the right to defend themselves and gain revenge for the broken contract.

"Do all Blood Drinkers know of this?"

"Apparently not." Hierarchy Clanman Thomas' frown spoke of his distaste as he took in the chaotic room. "I will pay for the damage and ensure that each leader knows about the agreement."

I nodded. "We will ensure that the Bombardians know as well."

"Hierarchy Clanman Thomas," Aidan hung his head a bit, but not much, "have you discovered another pairing like ours?"

Hierarchy Clanman Thomas dipped his head. "It has occurred twice before. My grandfather was there when the first pairing was discovered. It is how he found out about your kind and vice versa."

What a relief to know it happened before. That meant we would be able to find out how our pairing would work.

"They were compatible. In all ways. Most are also the Inamorato, like Commander Theodor is with you."

"Was the pairing with a Royal Leader?" I asked, hoping to gain more knowledge of what lay ahead of me and Aidan.

"Yes."

"Did they tell you about how it worked?" I cleared my throat, wishing I had a glass of water. The shift back had not only left me a bit hungry, but dry enough that my tongue stuck to the roof of my mouth.

"The pairing was a Protector."

Damn.

"Their pairing was a regular one. Their lives followed the same path that all Bombardians do. Their children were born with Royal Blood and no sign of Blood Drinkers blood or skills."

So . . . "Do you know which family the Royal Leader was from?"

"Afraid not."

Okay. Can't find out if it was mine or David's family line. The other three seats had changed family lines many times over the years. Mine and David's where the only two steady remaining Royal Leader's family.

"I believe your relationship will follow your way of life, Commander Theodor."

Did that mean mine and Aidan's would be like David and Bryan, Anthony and Larry's. Could I count on it? No. Truth was, Aidan and I was in new waters, just like David and Bryan had been when Bryan became sick. Least those two had relatives that could show them how to prepare for what lay ahead of them. I had no such. Discovering how a Protector and Royal Leader's pairing gave us an idea of what to look for, but . . . Keepers and Bombardians were different from Blood Drinkers and Keepers. In many ways.

"Why?" Aidan asked.

Hierarchy Clanman Thomas sighed and shrugged. "Gut."

"What do you think, honey?" I was leaning towards believing the Blood Drinker's leader. Things had gone like David and Bryan's. My Keeper chose to live my lifestyle. He had not given it a second thought. He was able to communicate with me like the Blood Drinkers, but . . . Some Bombardians gain such a link later in their relationships.

"I think he is right."

"Why?" David looked back at Cain and popped out of the room.

"David" I asked before Aidan could answer. "Do you need to tend to Bryan?"

"No." David gave me a weak smile but dipped his head.

"If you do then go."

"Cain can handle it."

"You sure?"

"Yes."

Cain popped back in and came up to David's side, whispering. David nodded and pulled a small pill bottle from his back pocket and handed it over. Cain left as quick as he had before.

"Aidan?" Caleb brought them back to the topic at hand.

"Right." Aidan shook his head. "It's a gut thing."

I whipped my head towards him as his voice quavered. *What is wrong?*

I . . . I do not . . . I don't quite . . .

Honey, do we need to excuse ourselves? I would extract us both in a blink if needed. I did not feel any danger, but I was clear my Keeper was concerned.

No. It's just . . . I don't know if I'm right or not.

Okay. Tell me and we can see how to proceed. I hoped I could do such. Then again . . . If not . . . it was no big deal. My cousins wouldn't get an answer. That simple.

I feel . . I smell . . . There is . . . I think I'm pregnant.

My knees all but buckled, but I forced them to hold me up. *Why?*

I . . . A Blood Drinker can . . . We have extremely sensitive noses. Most males can pick up on a different scent when their woman is expecting. Some can even tell the moment they are created. Is that common among your kind?

I'd heard a couple of Protectors say that. Larry had known. Bryan had felt . . . David had . . . Both of them have a deep connection with their twins. *I think it is.*

Then is it wise for us to let Hierarchy Clanman Thomas know.

Wasn't sure about that. I did not know the man. Did know that he would keep his Blood Drinkers inline. Yet . . . He'd failed to know how obsessed Lord Tang was with Connor. How he had broken the truce some time ago. Then again . . . He did not know about the truce.

Honey, do you know if he knew about Connor?

Aidan shook his head.

Then for now we keep this to ourselves.

I looked at Caleb and shook my head. Caleb picked up on my silent answer and moved onto another topic.

"Are you sure it was the first Royal Leader you made your deal with?"

Hierarchy Clanman Thomas nodded.

Why would he have kept that out of the book he started. He wouldn't have. That meant . . . "General."

"Yes, Commander Theodor."

"Stay with Aidan."

"Yes, Sir."

"David, I'll be right back."

Chapter 40

Theodor

I stood in the middle of my main house, sniffing. Perfect. No one was there. The lingering scents were hours old. I rushed down the hallway and into my office. I flipped the switch that opened the hidden cubby behind the fireplace. Inside sat four weathered leathered books. Each book held the first written account of our species. Since I was the eldest, they'd been passed into my keeping. I took it serious. My father had always kept them out in the open for anyone to see. That wasn't safe and I refused to be careless with them. The other four had printed out copies, but what I needed resided inside the original copy. I pulled the bottom book out and carefully flipped through each page until . . .

Damn it. Just what I thought.

Who had desecrated the book? Why? What had been so damn important to tear the information from their original history book. Edward wouldn't have. Who?

Nothing could be done. What had been torn away was gone. All left to do was set aside time for my cousins and I to sit and make another agreement with the Blood Drinkers. Add in how a pairing worked between the two species, especially between a Royal Leader and a Blood Drinker.

I zapped myself back, slipping Aidan against my side. Aidan slid closer, resting his head on my shoulder.

"What did you find?" Caleb went to the scratched up sofa, flopping down, making it creak. Damn. I loved that couch.

"There's a missing page in my book."

"Only one."

"Did not look for more. We can do that later." Hadn't really thought about it. Should have.

"What does that mean?" Aidan whispered into my ear, sending an electric current across my chest and down to my cock.

"Means . . ." I locked eyes with Hierarchy Clanman Thomas, "That we all need to sit down and make another agreement."

"Sounds good to me." Hierarchy Clanman Thomas snapped his fingers and the motionless Blood Drinkers faded into abyss."

"Neat." Aidan muttered.

"I hope," David moved in front of Hierarchy Clanman Thomas, blocking my view. "there will be no more invasions."

"There will not be." A slight bow accompanied Hierarchy Clanman Thomas.

"How did you and Lord Tang's men get by our wards?" Caleb crossed his legs.

"We have skills of our own." Hierarchy Clanman Thomas came into view when he moved next to Lord Tang, lifting him over his shoulder. "I'll let Aidan explain."

"Sir?" Aidan lifted his head. "I'm not sure how they done so either."

"You do know about our magical skills."

Aidan had mentioned such, but insinuated it was limited.

"Then you can explain that. They can infer how we did so."

Wouldn't need it explained. I already knew. They pulled from the elements, like we did.

"Don't need him to." David wiped his brown. "I felt the disturbance among Earth." He sighed. "Your kind need to respect Earth more than you do."

"Most do." Hierarchy Clanman Thomas bowed. "I can promise you very few of my subjects invades Earth without proper respect. Even I did so when I entered Commander Theodor's home."

"Not enough." David's legs gave way and he crumpled to the floor.

Caleb shot across the room, catching him before he hit the edge of the fireplace.

"What is wrong with him?" Aidan stiffened and slid out from under my arm.

"He overexerted himself." Bryan said from the doorway. "Move Cain."

When had Cain came into the room and knelt beside David? Had David known what was coming and called him? I would have called my General soon as I felt my energy draining.

"Royal Keeper Bryan, I have my orders."

I'd been right. Also knew that Bryan cared very little about orders. When the bomb went off, a few months back, Bryan had felt David's unease and took out his guards, rushing to his aid. Cain would not keep Bryan from David.

"Move, or I'll knock you aside."

"Let him by." I said. "He can help David more than anyone else."

"I can to." Hierarchy Clanman Thomas said.

"If you will drop your fire wall long enough for me to leave. I can quit holding onto Earth."

"Your using Earth weakened him?"

Had not considered such. I'd put blame on David's multiple shifts and pulling on multiple affinities. "It is down."

"Then I take my leave."

"Thank god." David took hold of Bryan and rubbed his stomach. "Safe and sound. Just like they should be."

"Did you know he was draining your energy?"

"Wasn't sure." David sighed and pushed up until he sat upright. "All I knew was that they pulled on Earth and she was not happy. Her distress took a toll on me. It was as if I was constantly pulling on her, draining her. Hierarchy Clanman Thomas paid proper respect, but it wasn't accepted. She felt the others that invaded and knew he was the leader of those who disrespected her."

Other words, she took from anyone who could aid her to break the unwanted hold on her.

"I'll kick his ass."

Leave it to Bryan to go defensive. Took all I could do not to laugh when Bryan went to stand, and David gripped him by the waist.

"It is fine. I just need to rest a bit."

"Is not."

"Baby, stay with me and help me regain my strength."

"Fine." Bryan's huff was cuter than the fire red face. "If he comes back without permission, I'll send some of my fury his way."

Bryan would. His anger was entertaining, but I knew the young man would do as he said. Bryan knew how to handle himself, with and without pulling on David's affinity.

"How will we contact him to setup a meeting?" Caleb retook his seat on the ruined sofa.

Wished it was the only thing destroyed. My recliner was in pieces and my built-in bookcase had been split in half. All my books were sprawled on the floor.

"I'll give him a call." Aidan's eyes took in the living room. "Least I was going to replace the furniture."

He was? I'd like most of the pieces in the living room. Didn't matter. I'd allow him to do whatever he wanted. That might have been why I snorted and kissed his cheek.

"I look forward to seeing how you decorate our home."

"I love to decorate."

It was going to be great to learn what my Keeper liked and disliked. More fun would come from discovering just who he was. First impression, and I don't think it was wrong, was that he was a hardcore leader. I think he was, but there was a softer side to him. A side that preferred to be led. Not that he would stand by and watch a fight. Nope, he'd jump into the fray and hold his own, but when it came right down to it, Aidan enjoyed the simpler life.

"Then," I took hold of his hand, "While we meet with Hierarchy Clanman Thomas, you can go shopping."

"You don't want me involved in the meeting?"

Ah, there was the leader side of him. Aidan was indeed a multifaceted person. "No."

"I don't mind going shopping. Used to do it a lot before I joined Lord Tang's clan. Long time since I went anywhere."

"Then you shop until your heart is satisfied." I waved my General over. "You appoint two guard to him for when he goes out."

"Done have, Commander."

"Good."

"I can . . ."

I kissed Aidan, silencing him. I made sure to inspect every inch of his mouth, then I kissed the tip of his nose before nuzzling his neck. "I know you can take care of yourself, but the guards will put me at ease."

"Okay."

Aidan's voice was strained, but he agreed. That eased the tension in my chest.

"Great. That's settled." Caleb stood. "Call and setup a time for him to come over."

My beast snarled and lifted a clawed hand.

"What?"

"I'm back. I'm the leader again."

"Right." Caleb shook his head. "Fine. I'm going to lay down for a bit."

"Sounds great to me." David ambled to his feet and took hold of Bryan's hand, leading them from the room.

"You want me to call him?"

"Please, honey."

"Consider it done."

Chapter 41

Aidan

Took me all of two minutes to call Hierarchy Clanman Thomas. He was more than pleased to meet with Theodor and his cousins. He even told me how pleased he was with how I handled the situation. Then he went on to tell me that he was disappointed that I would be leaving the Blood Drinker world. Not because he feared me giving away secrets, but he'd hoped I'd lead my own Clan. Come to find out, several of my fellow clan members had contacted him, requesting a change in leadership. Not that it was something that Hierarchy Clanman Thomas would have agreed to. He did not interfere with leaders, until they went overboard like Lord Tang had.

What shocked me more than anything during the call was that he revealed that he'd been watching my devotion to Lord Tang over the last ten years. I had never even known he was that involved in what took place among the clans. He always seemed to reside in the background until a situation like with Lord Tang arose.

Entire conversation gave me loads of information about how the inner workings of the Blood Drinker world truly function. Would have been nice to know all that years ago, but . . . Wasn't a concern of mine anymore. I had officially left the clan life. I was considered a lone Blood Drinker. That wasn't a bad thing. There were many of them among my kind. They did not have the support of a clan and made their way in life completely on their own. Not that, that would be a problem. What was, was that I had no way to support myself. I'd done nothing in life but be a guard to a leader. I'd worked hard to rise in the ranks of Lord Tang's clan. There was no working for a regular paycheck. Nope. Lord Tang had taken his money and invested it, gaining all the wealth it would take to lead the clan. We worked for him and he ensured that we all had we needed. Most Old Style Clans operated that way, but the few that existed were not as well off, failing to ensure that their clan prospered.

"You okay, honey?"

"Yeah."

"You lied to me. Why?"

What did I tell him? The truth did not sound good. It could make him despise me. Make him think me a freeloader. I did not want to be either, but . . . I was expecting. There was no way I could go into the world and find a job. I'd have to be kept hidden away until after the baby was born.

Hey, honey, Theodor using our mental link sent shivers over my body. *You can tell me anything. I do not want to pull it from your mind, but . . .*

He would if he had to. I would do the same to him.

"I'm not going to be able to aid you."

"Aid me? In what?"

"Anything. I'm simple a guard. It's all I know."

Theodor came up to me and tugged me into his chest. "I know life is going to be different than you are used to. Things will take time to fall into place. Until it does, we make our way through it.

"I have no way to give you anything monetary."

"Ah . . . You do not need to. We have more than enough money to live on for ten generations and I make more each day from my stocks."

"But . . ."

"Honey," Theodor lifted my chin so he could see my eyes. "I will be coming to you when I need to work through things. You are my rock. You are going to have your hands full with our little one."

I knew he was right, but . . .

"If it's such a bother, once our child is born, I will help you find a job. Not that I want you to work. It will make it hard to protect you from the shit storm that is coming our way when Larry announces the Bombardians to the world."

He was right. Them coming out to the public was going to send things into a tailspin. I could take care of myself, but . . . Being a Royal

Keeper meant . . . Not only human coming at me, but . . . Anyone who wanted to cause trouble for the Bombardians, or the Royal Leaders, would charge me. My being taken meant Theodor would do anything to get me back. I could not put myself into such a position. Nope. I had to ensure I was safe. At all times. Not just while I'm carrying. More so after I have our child. They would go after him or her with more gusto. I would be the last line of defense for our child and I was a formidable one. That wasn't something people would expect.

"You are right, babe. Just a bit in unknown waters and it is throwing me."

"Just think that you are aiding us with working out an agreement between our kind and yours. If things arise between Blood Drinkers and Bombardians then you will be our go-to guy. Long as it does not endanger you or our child."

"You are right." I ran my hand down Theodor's cheek. "I think Hierarchy Clanman Thomas knew I was expecting."

"Why you say that?"

"He told me to ensure I took care of myself."

"Seems logical since you were going to be leaving his reach."

"It was more the way he said it. A . . . Gut feeling."

"You think it is a bad thing?"

"No." My gut told me he was genuinely pleased. "Do you think what he knows about your kind and ours mixing is more than he let on?"

Theodor sighed and shrugged his shoulder. "I can ask him when we meet, but I am not sure if he would openly tell us. I would hope so, but . . . If I was in his spot, I'd be tentative about letting what I know get out. Then again . . . I would have been in his spot if someone had not desecrated a sacred book."

I couldn't see why my ultimate leader would withhold facts that effected one of his subjects. It seemed respectable and logical to enlighten everyone involved. Without facts, he'd leave me and Theodor floundering. I could not see what the point in doing so would be.

"I'm sure you will learn more during your meeting." I hoped.

Chapter 42

Theodor

The meeting with Hierarchy Clanman Thomas had not taken place, but the last three days had been nothing but one long ass meeting. We'd been secluded in the conference room from sunup to sundown. Might not have been that bad, but Bryan's sickness had gotten worse and the meetings kept being put on hold so David could go to his aid. David's uncle said the sickness had not been that bad for his Keeper and Larry's sickness was not that bad. Nor was Aidan's. Thankfully, he'd not been sick one time. Yet, neither of them were carrying twins. Clearly, we were in new water and had to just go with what came our way. One wave after another. Was not easy and bothersome when trying to nail down some major facts about what and when to release more information to the humans about the Bombardians. The world knew about them and things had become chaotic just like I knew it would. Some were giving the Destroyer's Hermitages a hard way to go and for the meantime we'd put the occupants of them on a type of house arrest. They were not allowed to leave unless their Bombardian was with them. The Bombardians that belonged to the Keeper or Protectors were taking turns guarding the house. We'd also limited the reasons that Bombardians could take their Keepers or Protectors out in public. We hoped by doing so that we decreased the destruction like we had when the Hermitages were first created. We'd lost many good Keepers and Protectors then, meaning many Bombardians became stuck in a half state. Many good men were lost.

We were on edge, not to mention our beast were pushing for control. Each one for a different reason, but none was worse than David's. Each time Bryan became distressed his claws extracted and his face contorted until he was at his Keeper's side. I think David's reaction to his sick Keeper was what added to Anthony and my beast becoming riled up. Franklin and Caleb seemed to be offended by the reaction of the humans, and that was riling up their other side. It was one or big stressful time. More than one situation came into play and we needed a break but there was not one in sight.

I simply wanted to go to Aidan and curl up for a day or two. Least Anthony was back to aid in helping make the more difficult decisions that rested at our feet. Only one good thing had come over the last three days. Aidan and Larry seemed to hit it off. Aidan and Tommy were more edgy around one another, but I was sure that would change once Tommy's fears for Bryan subsided. He was having as hard of a time with Bryan's constants sickness as David. The two were indeed closer than brothers. Not that it was a bad thing. Nope. It was a great thing. Even if he was taking him time to warm up to Aidan.

"Okay." David sighed and sat down. "We have about two hours before he wakes up."

"Then," I slid yellow notepads over to each one of them, "let's get down to business. We were about to write out what we think we should include in the meeting with Hierarchy Clanman Thomas."

"Still think," Anthony interjected, "that we should not be allowing them to keep themselves hidden."

Damn it. We'd been over that three times. Anthony's points were not going to change. Neither were mine. Not to mention, we'd taken a vote and it was four to one. Anthony was the only one that believed it would help our cause with the humans if another species were made known. I was not going to openly out another race. If someone had done so to us, we would have attacked them full force. I was not going to open the Bombardians up to such an act. Not when there was no need. The Blood Drinkers were no threat. All they wanted to do was live in peace and solitude. I was sure that a time would come when they would have to reveal themselves, but until then . . . It was no one's place to take that from them.

"Not our place." David said.

"Why not? They attacked us. Twice."

"We've been over this." I picked up my notepad. "We voted and the subject is over."

"Just wait." Anthony plucked his pen from the table. "Why are we each writing this down when we have already discussed what needs to be said?"

"Why are you being such a dick? "David threw his pen at Anthony, who ducked and snarled back. "Don't start with me."

That had been another issue. Anthony had been an ass since he rejoined them. I wasn't sure what was going on with the man, but his stubbornness was old.

"What is your deal?" I wrote out how I though the wording needed to be. "You know how we work. We have not changed since you left. We let you take care of your Keeper without interruption."

Something that never had occurred before. Royal Leader were always to be reachable. David, Franklin, and Caleb all agreed that it was best if Anthony focused on his Keeper while he struggled with his blood pressure issue. It was bothering him as much as Bryan's sickness was. Most of the time, Keepers and Protectors did not get sick, but pregnancy . . . Like any human or Protector's had side effects.

"You all handled everything while I was gone."

"Is that the issue?" I glanced up. "Did you think we would have to break our word to you and when we didn't you got pissed?"

"No." Anthony's wide-eyed expression pulled a chuckle from Caleb, who had remained quiet every time Anthony went on another tirade."

"Then what is it?" I tore the sheet of paper off and folded it, sliding it to the pile in the middle of the table. "We have less than an hour to get this wording nailed down."

"That's just it." Anthony dropped his tablet onto the table. "We are bending over backwards for this guy like we did the humans when we first negotiated with the humans."

"What?" David tossed his folded sheet into the middle of the others. "That was different."

"Is it?" Anthony shrugged. "They did not openly admit we were a different race. They created another cover story to hide what we were from the world. It wasn't until Larry helped us that we fully become known to the humans. Even now they are openly seeking ways to find out who are Bombardians and hurt them or get at them by hurting the ones living in the Destroyer's Hermitage. What are we going to do when these Blood Drinkers decide they dislike our agreement with their leader? What will we do if they break their word to us and go to the humans and reveal all they know about us?"

Valid points, but it went both ways. We were not only trusting the Blood Drinkers not to run to the humans with our secrets, but they were putting all their eggs in a basket that we would not tell the humans about them. Hierarchy Clanman Thomas was trusting us to keep our word. In return he deserved the same trust. Did he not?

"Hierarchy Clanman Thomas is an honorable man." Aidan said from the doorway. "I am sure he has considered this as much as you have. I know I have no say in what you guys decide and I don't want to, but I can say that once Hierarchy Clanman Thomas gives his word he keeps it."

"How can you say that?" Anthony crossed his arms, pulling a small snarl from me, which he ignored. "You are just another subject of his."

"I am more than that."

He was? News to me. What had my Keeper kept from me? Had he done so on purpose? Was it an oversight? I'd know he'd been able to reach out to him quickly and directly. Most leaders had people to go through before you got to the main guy. I'd put that up to his father working for the Hierarchy Clanman.

"I am his great-great-grandson."

"Damn." David said.

"Fuck." Caleb chimed in.

"Really?" Anthony sat back and stared at Aidan, earning a deeper and harsher snarl from me. "Sorry." He lifted his hands. "It's just you said he was Connor's relative. Last living one."

"That's not what I said."

"You've got it mixed up." David snorted. "He said Connor was Lord Tang's last living relative."

"Oh." Anthony frowned and stared down at his crossed arms. "Sorry."

"Did Lord Tang know about this?" David turned his chair around. "I mean . . . Losing Connor and Robyn was not something a leader should have flipped out over."

"No. That was because I helped Connor sneak away and left myself."

"Honey, you sure about that."

"Yes." Aidan came to my side and wrapped his arms around my neck. "No one knows my connection to my great-great-grandfather. It is safer for him if all thinks he has no family."

"Makes sense." Caleb tapped his pen against the table. "Gives no one a reason to openly attack you. Hierarchy Clanman Thomas is keeping his family safe. You three do the same by putting guards on your Keepers."

He was right. We did all we could to keep our loved ones safe. Not to mention our homes a secret. The more Bombardians that knew of our locations and family the less they could hold over us. Over the years some of those have been revealed. It was the only reason we kept the ones born with royal blood a secret. The ones on the list would live a life of constant fear of attack if we did not. If the Ghioulians had known who to eliminate before they attacked the Royal Leaders . . . Would have been a bigger disaster than it was. More than two lives would have been lost. No replacement for leaders meant an easier takeover.

"No offense," Anthony slid his sheet of paper to the middle of the table, "I still think we are taking a big risk."

"We might be." I gathered the five sheets of paper, "but it is the best option at this time. So . . ." He unfolded one sheet and read it. "We have done voted and the majority agreed that this new agreement is the best approach. That's the end of it. All we have to do is come up with the right wording." I unfolded the second sheet and then the others. "Looks like most of us have the same idea." I laid all five piece of paper side by side. "Come take a look and read them for yourselves. See if you agree with one more than the others. Then we can make adjustments from there." I wrapped an arm around Aidan and led him to the side of the room. "Did you need something, honey?"

"Just to say bye before me and Larry left for the mall."

"I could go for a quick taste of you." I leaned in and claimed his lips, hard and rough, making the kiss as deep as possible.

"Damn." Aidan's eyes held a haze to them as he gave some kind of goofy smile. "That was . . . Amazing. I'll come tell you bye more often if it gets me such a deep kiss."

"You earned more than that for being so open with my cousin."

"I understand his fears." He nuzzled my neck. "I'm sure the other have it as well, but they have seen Hierarchy Clanman Thomas in action, giving them a chance to gage him for themselves. Anthony has not."

"You are right." I nodded to my General when he came in with Aidan's guards at his heels. "I think your guards are ready to go."

"You sure you don't want me to stay for the rest of the meeting?"

"I am." I gave him a light kiss. "Go. Enjoy yourself."

Chapter 43

Theodor

White window curtains were drawn, blocking out some of the mid-day sun. One thing I'd learned about the Blood Drinkers were that they did not sleep during the day, but the sun drained their blood reserves, meaning the more they were in the sun the more blood they required. It's why Aidan had chosen to go in BASS, Bad Ass Shit-Kicker Security. Not that my General would have let him go in any other vehicle. It was the one vehicle that could pretty much take anything and had pure black out, bullet proof windows. Even the outside of the military style vehicle was bullet-proof. Only one thing had taken it down one time. Then it had been attacked by a large group of Ghioulians, renegade Mélange, that had followed a leader dead-set on eliminating all five Royal Leaders.

"He's going to be fine." David patted me on the shoulder as he walked by. "You sure all five of us need to be in the room?"

I nodded, watching as BASS turned left, heading toward town. "It's best if he sees a solid front."

"He's right." Caleb came in, taking the recliner next to me, kicking his legs up. "It's best if Hierarchy Clanman Thomas knows how strong we are as a team. He needs to know we work as one, whereas he is only one."

"We are not going to have any trouble from him."

I turned and made my way over to the last recliner, since Anthony and Franklin had taken residence on the sofa. Thanks to Aidan we had an insight into best how to approach his great-great-grandfather. He told us that a stuffy conference room wasn't wise. He preferred a more at ease atmosphere. With that in mind we rearranged my living room so that the furniture was in a circle. Gave everyone a line of sight, even if guards had to stand the entire time. I knew me and my cousins and our beast would not allow anyone to have higher ground. Even if it was only in a standing position. Our beast would have preferred them all to have their backs against the wall, preventing others from sneaking up on us. Not that I expected such to occur in my . . . Then again . . . There'd been multiple invasions several days ago. The circle meant that Me, Caleb, and David could watch the backs of Anthony and Franklin's while they watched ours. We'd also made it so that Hierarchy Clanman Thomas had to sit between me and David, putting his back against the fireplace. I was sure that Hierarchy Clanman Thomas would know we arranged the place on purpose.

"Commanders," Cain came in from the hallway, stopping with his hands behind his back. "He is at the front gate."

Time was here. I took in a deep breath and let the outer circle of fire prevention drop. "Have my General escort him in."

"Yes, Commander Theodor." Cain spun on his heels and marched out of the room.

"Thought you said Tommy mellowed him out." I groaned when David rolled his eyes at me.

"He has." David huffed. "Cain has two modes. Relaxed and out of work and work. He is the best I've seen at switching back and forth from one to the other. He does it in a blink of an eye."

"I've noticed." Caleb pushed the leg rest back into its down position.

"Royal Leaders," Hierarchy Clanman Thomas gave them each a small bow.

All five of us stood and returned the jester. I motioned toward the empty chair. "Let's all sit. Would you like something to drink? Eat?"

Another fact I'd learned about Blood Drinkers was that they ate and drank like humans, even though they required blood daily, sometimes more depending on their sun exposure and their body make up. Like humans and Bombaridans some required more food than others.

"I am fine, but thanks." Hierarchy Clanman Thomas appeared to float over to the chair. I would have believed he did, if his feet had not made small indentions on the freshly vacuumed carpet. "I had hoped to see Aidan today."

"He has gone on a shopping trip."

"He has?"

"Yes." I sat back down. "He seemed like a child who won all the chocolate in the world."

"Most likely did." Hierarchy Clanman Thomas crossed his ankles. "Lord Tang did not allow his subject to leave his domain."

"Why did you allow him to live such a secluded life?" David rocked back and forth, which I knew calmed his beast, meaning David was stressed. Nothing new. Bryan and his upcoming twins had him on edge since the discovery of them.

"I do not tell my Blood Drinkers how to live."

"Do you still believe that it is a good idea?" Caleb's at ease tone had Hierarchy Clanman Thomas' eyebrow lifting.

I hadn't expected my cousins to be anything but their normal self. We'd agreed to be who we were. Not to hide how we lived and dealt with matters.

"To some extent." Hierarchy Clanman Thomas sighed. "I am afraid that I have only two other clans that seclude themselves. Even they do not go to the extent that Lord Tang did."

"He has been dealt with?" Anthony's question pulled Hierarchy Clanman Thomas' attention, but he did not remained focus on him.

His eyes diverted back to me. I wasn't following what the dulling red eyes meant, but I was sure it was not good. Did not take me long to find out the reason behind the unease flowing through the air.

"May I ask who he is?"

Right. Anthony had not been there when Lord Tang invaded.

"I apologize." I waved towards Anthony. "Commander Anthony was not with us the other day."

"May I ask why?"

"It is personal." Anthony crossed his arms and sat forward.

I expected a rejection to be voiced at the daring tone, but the Blood Drinker gave a shrug and moved their meeting along.

"I am sure by now Aidan has told you his and mine connection."

I nodded.

"Good. I do not have to." Hierarchy Clanman Thomas' shoulder relaxed and his eyes went back to a bright red. A look I'd seen on Aidan's face since the night we'd first made love. "I am sure that you all desire a new agreement between us. Is that correct?"

"It is." I replied. "As you found out the other day, we were not aware one existed."

"I am not quite sure . . ."

I held my hand up when Caleb went to speak. One thing I knew about him was that when he was anxious or nervous, he chose the worst manner to respond. I wasn't sure what had caused his knee to start bouncing, but David had picked up on it and stiffened as well. Franklin either picked up on one, or both, and began scanning the room with intense filled eyes. Wasn't sure if Anthony took note, but he had gone still as a board. I took in a couple of deep breaths and gaged my surroundings.

Hierarchy Clanman Thomas seemed content and in control. Appeared he had not felt any disturbance, so what had made my cousins go on alert.

"David?"

"Not sure, Theodor."

"Caleb?"

He shook his head.

"Franklin?"

"Me either."

I stood and moved to the window, gaining a perfect line of sight of my General, who spun to face me. I tossed my head towards the metal gate that protected my home. It was far enough away from the house that no one could see what was going on behind it, but still within Bombardians' view range.

"Hierarchy Clanman Thomas," I took in the line of Bombardians gathering on the other side of the gate. "I am afraid you will have to give us a few minutes to tend to another matter." I did not wait for an answer. Simply headed for the door. I knew my cousins were at my back.

Chapter 44

Aidan

"This has been amazing."

"Best enjoy it now." Larry fingered the strap of the large plastic bag that held the massive number of books he bought.

I knew nothing about what they were, but he said they were the material he needed to research how to help other Keepers and Bombardians cope with the screw up his father had created. It wasn't until he told me that he was the President's son that it registered with me. Theodor had mentioned that there'd been some humans attacking Destroyer Hermitages and outwardly seeking Bombardians. Made me glad that the Blood Drinker had never came public. If the humans feared people with a wolf inside them, they'd hate and shoot to kill someone who needed blood as well as food to survive.

"Once I start to show, I'll be stuck in the house even more than I am now."

Went for me as well. I was expecting, a fact that I'd yet to grasp the enormity of, but one that I was thrilled about. Never really considered having children, but it would be nice to continue mine and Theodor's family line. Just wish I knew if the child would be more Blood Drinker or more Bombardian. Or even half and half. For all I knew, it would take on the Bombardian aspect. Not that I minded that. Theodor was amazing. Past involved Protectors, I'm a Keeper. Would that make a difference?

"What is that?" Larry leaned over as Alvin, one of the Combatants that was upfront, asked.

Theodor? I automatically sought him through our mental link, hoping to ensure myself that he was okay. Not to mention that my great-great-grandfather was.

I'm fine, honey. The soothing voice allowed me to take a deep breath.

What is going on?

Not quite sure, but I am about to find out. Are you guys outside?

Yes.

My General will make sure things are taken care of. You and Larry just sit tight for a bit.

Is my . . .

Your great-great-grandfather is in the living room. He's safe and sound. I promise.

Thanks, babe.

"Royal Keepers," Alvin faced us through the middle of the seats. "We will sit tight until I get a text from my General."

"Is that more protesters?" Larry sighed and muttered how he hoped it wasn't and that if so, Anthony's cousins were going to hate him.

"Hey," I took hold of his hand, squeezing until he looked up at me. "Those guys could not hate you for anything. You know that."

"I was the one that went live about them."

"Was it not them that wanted you to?"

"Yes, but . . . I delivered the news."

Aidan didn't know the other that well, especially Larry's Royal Leader, but he knew that none of them would blame the one that did as they requested.

Babe?

What's wrong, honey?

Larry's blaming himself about the protesters.

They are not protesters.

What are they?

Bombardians.

Shit. That could be worse. Bombardians had been working overtime to protect their Keeper and Protectors. Some even guarding the homes they resided in. Others had confined their other halves to their homes for the safety. Even then, some of those homes had been attacked.

"They are not protesters." I gave Larry a wisp of a smile, or I hoped that's how it came out.

"How do you know that?"

"I have a deeper connection with Theodor than most Keepers."

"Because of being a Blood Drinker?"

"Yes."

"Then what are they?"

"Bombardians." Alvin supplied. "They will not harm any of us."

"How sure are you of that?" Larry's voice wavered and he began rubbing his temple.

I knew that the man had been having difficult time with his pregnancy and that's why him and Anthony had been MIA for the last few weeks. They wanted him kept calm as possible. Theodor mentioned something about blood pressure spiking and causing passing out. I wasn't sure how to aid the man and was not sure if the Combatants did or not. There was only one from Anthony's team with them.

Theodor?

What honey?

I think Anthony's Combatant might need to zap Larry into the house.

What's going on?

He's rubbing his temple and his face is paling. His voice is wavering. He wanted to know how sure Alvin was that the Bombardians would not attack us.

Okay. Thanks for letting me know.

It was less that a second later that Anthony appeared in the middle of BASS and faded with Larry as quick. I barely got two breaths taken.

"You okay, Royal Keeper Aidan?"

"Yes, Alvin."

"Let me know if that changes."

"I will."

Theodor had enough to deal with. He did not need me losing my shit. Not that I would. Was use to hard situation. It came along with being second in command to Lord Tang. Or it had when I first took over the spot. Back then Lord Tang got into some major scrapes with other Clans.

I scooted to the middle of the seat, gaining a better line of sight out the front window. I set the bags that I had kept with me aside and leaned forward. Waiting.

Chapter 45

Theodor

"What is going on?" Franklin asked for the fourth time as we made our way outside. "Hello, Theodor."

I kept on walking. I had no idea why there was a hoard of Bombardians outside my house. Nor how they found me. Looked as if security needed beefing up on all of our houses. Sure was something I would take care of soon. I had a Keeper, a pregnant one, to protect.

"David," I looked over my shoulder, catching sight of a frown marring his face. "What is it?"

"I think I may know why these Bombardians have shown up."

"Explain."

"Cain has received reports about uproar among the Bombardians who have Keeper and Protectors in the Destroyer's Hermitages."

The attacks. They'd been quite a few of them over the last few weeks. Even some Bombardian homes had been attacked. Some of the homes destroyed did not belong to Bombardians.

"We put guards around them. Bombardians volunteered to do so. Not like we didn't deal with attacks when they were first created."

"From what Cain told me, the attacks were coming more frequent and grew in violence."

Shit. Keepers and Protectors had been beaten within an inch of their lives when the Cult had been created. Had taken multiple orders and putting Bombardians in cells for days at a time to control them. Not for punishment, but to keep them from retaliating on those who harmed theirs.

"Any deaths?" Caleb came to my side, taking in the mass. "That's a lot at your gate when no one should have known where this place is."

Agreed. Their shouts for a Royal Leader not only echoed in my mind but shot rods through my entire body. It was as if their combined voices ricocheted off his home. Rich, thick rage flowed from the other side of the barricade. Even . . .

"Death."

Theodor?

Who knew my name could create ease through my beast.

I'm fine, honey.

What is going on?

Not quite sure, but I am about to find out. Are you guys outside? If so, they needed to stop the entire shitstorm before it happened.

Yes.

My General will make sure things are taken care of. He best at least. *You and Larry just sit tight for a bit.*

"I smell it." Anthony took in a deep breath. "Are we going to be facing off with Mélange?"

Is my . . .

Your great-great-grandfather is in the living room. He's safe and sound. I promise.

Thanks, babe.

Babe?

What's wrong, honey?

Larry's blaming himself about the protesters.

They are not protesters.

What are they?

Bombardians.

I hoped that all they were, but . . . If someone's Keeper or Protector had been killed there was a huge chance a Mélange resided among the crowd. Then again . . . If he was allowed to gain revenge . . . He might be fine.

"No use standing out here." Caleb waved at the guard next to the gate.

The Combatant shouted for the Bombardians to back up. I was just about to move off the porch when Aidan reached out.

Theodor?

What honey?

I think Anthony's Combatant might need to zap Larry into the house.

What's going on?

He's rubbing his temple and his face is paling. His voice is wavering. He wanted to know how sure Alvin was that the Bombardians would not attack us.

Okay. Thanks for letting me know.

"Anthony, go get Larry. He's in distress."

"What? How . . ."

Anthony faded away and back before another breath was taken. He rushed Larry inside and remained there. Just like I expected him to. We did not need his mind split between his Keeper and the events taking place outside. If we lost his Keeper or their child . . . things might go south inside the gates as well as outside.

The crowd grew quiet as David, Franklin, Caleb and I came to stand in between the gate doors. We left enough room for them to shut immediately if the need arose.

The first three Bombardians dropped to their knees. A generous show of kindness, one we did not require, but it showed loyalty to us and their willingness to obey. Each Bombardian knew we did what was best for them in the long run. New we would hear them out and take into account what they said. Not to mention try and find solution for what bothered them.

"Commander Theodor," my General came up to my side, pointed at each guy as he spoke. "This is Ramon, George, and Lee. They have Protectors stationed at the Dallas Hermitage."

Wasn't sure how my General knew so much about them, but it was clear he'd been in contact with them before I felt them outside.

"Gentlemen." I nodded at each and then at the group behind them. "What can we do for you?"

"Commanders, we are sorry for showing up without proper notice." Ramon lowered his head. "I know it is unlawful for me to know where you live, but I felt I had no choice."

"Why is that?" I scanned the group, taking in the entire second row of Bombardians. They shifted from foot-to-foot but made no sudden move forward. They remained tight lipped and allowed the ones who they must have appointed as the spokesmen to answer.

"As I told your General, the Dallas Hermitage was attacked for the third time last night. My Protector is only alive because of my slight talent of Earth." Other words, Ramon was at least in the top twenty percent of Bombardians that carried royal blood. Top thirty percent held the ability to tap into their affinity in small bouts. "George and Lee were not as lucky. The fire cocktail tossed into the house landed in their Protectors' beds."

Shit. They would not have had time to pop in and retrieve them like Anthony had been able to Larry. Life being snuffed out by any means was horrible, but burning to death . . . I knew how painful it could be. I had not been set on fire, but every time I used my affinity, I felt the fire bubbling under my skin. If not for my affinity I would burn from the inside out.

"How," David came to my side, "many others were harmed?"

"Half of the Protector were injured. Four died."

Wasn't up to date on how many lived in the Dallas Hermitage, so I looked to David, he kept records on every last aspect. The man had files on each Bombardian around the world. Not to mention how they were connected to each other. He was the most organized Royal Leader who lived. It had come in handy over the last few months.

"Fifteen harmed." David nodded at the kneeling men.

"That is correct, Commander David." George squeaked out.

"He's barely holding on." Franklin went up to him and rested a hand on the top of his head. "Let me ease you some."

I stood in awe when a whiff of vanilla and lavender consumed the air. I knew Spirit was the one connected to death, but I never saw it used to soothe before.

"That will not last for long, but it will help you get through what you came to ask of us."

"Thank you, Commander Franklin." Lee bumped George's shoulder. "Him and Camellia had been bound together for over forty years."

Long time for combining. Longer a couple were together the stronger their connection was. I had heard my father mention how he pretty much lived in my mother's mind. My parents had been paired together since she turned eighteen.

"How long were you with your Protector?" I asked.

"Ten years, Sir."

"And you, Ramon?"

"Five short years."

Explained why he hadn't gone straight to Mélange. Also showed how much restraint and control over their beast that George and Lee had. We would have lost them immediately if not.

"Commanders," Ramon lifted his head, but did not meet their eyes. "What can we do to guard our Protectors and the Keepers. I know they live in different Hermitages, but they all deserve our upmost protection. They ground us."

Wish there was a solid answer. I did not have one. Things were still in an uproar among the humans. Larry's father, President Wells, had dragged his feet and forced us to go public without his backup. That was making things go at a slower progression than we'd hoped for. It had also, most likely, caused the quicker uproar among the humans. They saw the footage firsthand. No government official coming forward . . . created a tailspin worse than a F-5 tornado. That was bound to be making it harder for some to try and adjust. Not that it would matter much. Majority of the humans would only see us as a threat and try to combat it before it became a major one. Entire situation had become so stressful for Larry that Anthony secluded him. From what little I knew about Larry he was the type of man that would blame himself for the trouble coming our way simply because he voiced the truth. It was not his idea. We asked him to do so, but he would not view it that way. Larry was an honorable man. One who believed in the truth and lived to aid others. He was trying his damnedest to ensure help for those of our kind that required it.

Me running into my Keeper had slowed me down. I'd not paid as much attention as I normally would have. I had depended on Franklin, Caleb, and David. Not my fault, either.

A murmur of voice grew, which had me lifting my hand up. Agitated Bombaridans wasn't something we needed.

"For now," I looked at my cousins, getting a slight nod of agreement for me to take the rein. "We will increase the round the clock protection on the Destroyer's Hermitages. At least one or two, depending on the size of the hermitage, will have a Bombardian inside. He will reside in the living room, therefore avoiding the distraction of his Keeper or Protector. The Protector or Keeper that runs the home will decide the scheduled of each Bombardian. And each one will have to guard inside as well as outside." I knew it was not a foolproof plan, but it would at least put them at ease. I hoped. "My General will send out this issue today. While this is going on, we will double our efforts to get the human government to join us in enlightening the world to our kind. It is not much of a solution, but like when the Red Hooded Guy was created, we have to do our best to protector ourselves and our Keepers and Protectors. We will put video surveillance outside the Hermitages and take them to the law. I am not sure how much good it will do, but we will not give into our baser needs and automatically attack. It will not aid us in any way. Overall, it will make things worse. As of right now, we still have the law on our side. There has been no vetoing the Cult aspect, so we will continue to use that to assist us." There was some nods and some murmur of disgust, which both I expected, but no one seemed to throw a fit about my plan. "For now, go back to your homes. Give us time to gain control of the situation. We are working hard as we can on the state of things. I promise." Not hard enough, but that would have to change. "George. Lee. Do you need to be assigned to a house for your own safety?"

The two exchanged a look and then looked back at some of the men in the first row. "Can we all be put in the same area?"

"By all means." David snapped his finger and Cain popped in.

"Yes, Commander David."

"Take the Bombardians that lost their Protectors in the Dallas Hermitage to the home in our hometown."

Each Royal Leader had one house for those who lost, or was refused by their other half, near their home."

Cain approached George and Lee, resting a hand on their shoulder, while the rest of the guys moved up behind them. Then they were all gone.

The rest of the Bombardians disappeared, leaving the driveway clear. I waved the BASS in, watching as it drove ahead of us.

"We have to finish up with Hierarchy Clanman Thomas." I spun on my heels and headed back to the house. Once again, I knew my cousins were behind me.

Chapter 46

Aidan

One by one the crowd faded into emptiness, or I should say, a greenish-bluish mist. I'd seen the aspect many times after a group of Lord Tang's guards left suddenly. Thing was, I'd always thought it was just magic, but according to Theodor and David our skills were pulled from Earth. David also swore that we did not pay enough respect to Earth, which weakened him greatly when Lord Tang brought his goons to attack the Royal Leaders. More so when, Hierarchy Clanman Thomas showed up to end Lord Tang's tirade of hatred.

"We're moving, sit back, please."

I sat back and watched as we drove through the metal gates. I watched as we passed Theodor and the others. Once BASS was by them, they began heading towards the house.

"Leave the bags."

"No." I was not going to have people wait on me. I had not let them carry them to the car to start with. I might have to have guards while out and about, but that did not mean they were my slaves.

I grabbed up the four huge bags and made sure I had a tight grip on the heaviest two. I was about to push the door open when someone did so. First thing I saw was a large hand, then the sexiest face in the world.

"Hey, babe." I shook my head at him and lifted the bags. "Hands are full."

"They can bring them in."

"Nope. I got them." I slid out and his arms were around me before I could even take a breath. His hand ran up the back of my shirt and came to rest on the middle of my back. He leaned down and took my lips, causing my knees to buckle.

"Damn, babe."

"Missed you."

"Me too." I snuggled into his chest, letting his warmth soak into my cooler skin. "Everything okay with the Bombardians?"

"Smoothed over. We've got lots to do before our people will be completely safe from the humans."

"More violence?"

I hated the idea that people were being harmed for being who they were. It only made me grateful that my kind was not out. I was sure they'd do more than attack Blood Drinkers. They would murder us on spot.

"Don't worry. We faced similar when they created the cult. We will survive this as well."

"Hierarchy Clanman Thomas still waiting?"

"Yes. I've got to get back to him. The others are just inside waiting for me to reassure my beast that you are fine."

"Fine and full of goodies."

"I see that."

"More to come tomorrow."

"Deliveries. Oh boy."

"Did I do wrong?"

"Did you get what you wanted?"

I grinned at him, nodding.

"Then there is nothing wrong. I can't wait to hear all about it." He kissed me lightly then released me. "Take that stuff to our room and sort it out so I can look when I'm done with Hierarchy Clanman Thomas."

I tightened the hold on the bags when Alvin reached for them. I gave Theodor a light kiss back then stepped around him, heading inside, nodding hello to the other four.

Chapter 47

Theodor

"Sorry for that." I walked over to my seat and waved for Hierarchy Clanman Thomas to retake his seat.

"I hope everything is all right." His voice was sincere, and he did not ask any other questions. "I am surprised that so many Bombardians know where you live."

Appeared that only one had. His being a royal blood carrier gave him some advantages, but he did break the law by bringing so many to my home. It would be the last time that I'd be able to use this place. I'd have to sale it and buy another in the area, since I have a confinement home nearby. Then again . . . I would not sale it. I would keep it for one of the non-emergency homes. After all, Aidan had just bought all kinds of stuff to remodel the place. I was not going to take his fun from him. He had worn the hugest smile when he climbed out of BASS. I'd let him do whatever he wanted, as long as it did not endanger him. Still, none of this could be discussed among mixed company.

"Let's get our agreement written down and placed back in our Bombardians Rule Book."

"What did you have in mind?" Hierarchy Clanman Thomas crossed his ankles and focused on a photo that hung over the top of my doorway. "That is one of . . . He gave you permission to hang that?"

I grinned back at the newest photo in my house. Aidan had insisted it be hung where he could see it from the love seat that sat beside the fireplace. He also stated that it would be the perfect spot for Hierarchy Clanman Thomas to see it when he sat down. I'd not understood why but did not question it. Just told him to put his things where he wanted them. He'd not brought many things. Nor had Hierarchy Clanman Thomas sent much to him. I'd asked him why and received an answer that I'd not expected.

Apparently, Lord Tang did not allow much personal items. Photos where one of the things the man allowed. Even then, Aidan did not have but five. There were a few whatnots and lots of clothes. Not as much as I had, but still quite a bit.

"Aidan insisted." David said.

"I approve." Hierarchy Clanman Thomas nodded at me. "He loves your dearly or he would not have placed his family among your living area. That is major."

"Major?" I'd just loved how Aidan made himself at home.

"Yes, but . . . He can explain later. For now . . ."

"Right." I kicked my legs out. "We do not want our races to be complete strangers. So . . . We thought our agreement should state that Bombardians will do everything in their power to keep the humans, or others, from finding out about your kind. That mingling together is not against the law, long as your secret is protected."

Hierarchy Clanman Thomas rubbed his chin, nodding. "My kind will not avoid enlightening your kind to our status around you."

"In other words," David leaned forward, "we both will be respectful to both kinds and do our best not to step on the other's toes."

"Right." Caleb shook his head. "That is what we are saying, but it is not going to be as simple to write down."

"It is." I snatched the notepad I'd written out what I'd hope we would agree on down. I was nothing but prepared. Okay, it'd been David's idea to come it with something written down. Not to mention, Aidan said it would go a long way to show Hierarchy Clanman Thomas how series we were about the agreement. I tossed the pad over to Caleb. "Read."

Caleb nodded a couple of times then dropped the pad onto the table. "Okay."

I'd known the late night of work would pay off. As much as I'd wanted to remain in bed with Aidan, I'd slipped away after he fell asleep. My wording had ensured that both sides had the anonymity we desired but had the right to mix among each other if we wanted to. If I was paired with Aidan, then how many other Bombardians had Keeper or Protectors among the Blood Drinkers. Also ensured that there'd be no hiding from each other and that we could both offer aid if a situation arose. I wanted to reassure Hierarchy Clanman Thomas knew his kind had a friend among the Bombardians. One he could call upon for aid. And . . . Considering the situation that showed up on my doorstep we might just need some behind the scene help. Then again . . . Blood Drinker aid in dealing with the humans might not be wise. It might get them outed. Not what I wanted to happen.

"You with us cousin?" David tight voice drew me away from the track my mind was heading down.

"Yes.

"Do you agree with Hierarchy Clanman Thomas adding in that any request regarding a matter involving a Blood Drinker goes to him first?"

"Of course." I'd expect no less. Same should go for Bombardians. "Same for us."

"Yes." Hierarchy Clanman Thomas picked up a pen and scribbled his name across the bottom of the pad. He passed it to me. "All we need is you and your cousins' signature."

I quickly signed my name and passed it to David. Took less than a minute to make its way back to me. I stood and nodded at them. "I'll go make a copy."

"No need." Hierarchy Clanman Thomas snapped his fingers and a sheet of paper appeared in his hand. "I have a duplicate."

"Neat."

I whipped my head around, smiling at Aidan. "Honey, you get it all sorted out?"

Aidan came up to my side and slipped his arm around me. "Yes. Quicker than I expected. Most is coming tomorrow."

"Great." I squeezed him closer. "You want to sit down?"

"Are you guys done?"

"We are." Hierarchy Clanman Thomas stood and held his hand out to Aidan. "You have found a very generous and caring Inamorato. I know you will be taken care of. With that and a word of warning to your Bombardian." He shifted his full red blood eyes to mine. "You hurt him and my full furry will be brought down onto you. We clear?"

"We are." I bowed. "I willingly give my life for his."

"Then . . ." Hierarchy Clanman Thomas gave a small tilt of his head. "I leave you to your life."

No other parting words were said. He simply left the way he came in.

"See why he is in charge." David snorted. "He has Earth's full backing when he pays proper respect."

"Good to know." I nuzzled Aidan's neck. "Want to go and show me what you brought home?"

"Would love to."

"Why not just say you want some time to nook?" Caleb chuckled. "Don't forget we've got to get Anthony and go over the issues facing us with the humans."

"I haven't forgotten. Just want some time to start a life with my Keeper."

"Then go have fun. I'm going to go aid Bryan."

"Me and Caleb . . ." Franklin huffed, "will sit here and twiddle our thumbs."

"You will find your soon. I'm sure of it." I said as I led Aidan back to our room.

"Ready to start our life?"

"More than."

Last thing I heard from the living room was Caleb reminding me we had to plan two pledging ceremonies."

We did, but first Aidan and I needed time together.

# # #

Dear Reader,

Thank you for reading Marked One Theodor and Aidan. Hope you enjoyed and were able to let your imagination soar with each word you read. If you did, make sure you keep an eye out for Franklin's story.

I love to hear from my readers; therefore, I answer all my emails. I'm a firm believer that you can't better yourself if your errors aren't pointed out. So, feel free to contact me and let me know about any you spot or what you thought about the book.

Please keep reading and letting your imagination soar.

Julia Matthews

Website: www.juliamatthews.webs.com[1]

Blog Site https://juliamatthewssp.blogspot.com/

Email: julia.matthews5@gmail.com

1. http://www.juliamatthews.webs.com

OTHER BOOKS AVAILABLE BY JULIA MATTHEWS

MOON CALLED
HUMAN-SKINNED WOLVES BOOK 1
RED MOON CIRCLE
HUMAN-SKINNED WOLVES BOOK 2
WOLF CLUB
HUMAN-SKINNED WOLVES BOOK 3
HIDDEN WOLF
HUMAN-SKINNED WOLVES BOOK 4
COLLAR OF TRUTH
HUMAN-SKINNED WOLVES BOOK 5
MERCIFUL WOLF
HUMAN-SKINNED WOLVES BOOK 6
WOLF REVELATION
HUMAN-SKINNED WOLVES BOOK 7
JOURNEY TO A MATE
BOOK 1 OF JOURNEY SERIES
(CO-WRITTEN BY VICKIE MATTHEWS)
ANYTHING FOR A MATE
BOOK 2 OF JOURNEY SERIES
CLAIMING MY MATE
BOOK 3 OF JOURNY SERIES
JOURNEY REVEALED
BOOK 4 OF JOURNEY SERIES
WITCH & WOLF
(CO-WRITTEN BY VICKIE MATTHEWS)
WARLORD DEMISE
UNRAVELLING
REVEALED BY LOVE
AWAKENING LOVE
MARKED ONES DAVID AND BRYAN
BOOK 1 OF MARKED ONES SERIES

MARKED ONES ANTHONY AND LARRY
BOOK 2 OF MARKED ONES SERIES

www.ingramcontent.com/pod-product-compliance
Lightning Source LLC
LaVergne TN
LVHW050540160826
845677LV00011B/2115

* 9 7 9 8 2 3 0 9 1 1 4 1 8 *